Also by Wayne Koestenbaum

The Cheerful
Scapegoat

Published by Semiotext(e)
PO BOX 629, South Pasadena, CA 91031
www.semiotexte.com

Cover: Wayne Koestenbaum, *Evening Quartet with Henrique*, 2019.

Design: Hedi El Kholti
ISBN: 978-1-63590-144-3

Distributed by the MIT Press, Cambridge, MA, and London, England.
Printed and bound in the United States of America.

The Cheerful Scapegoat

Fables

Wayne Koestenbaum

semiotext(e)

for Steven Marchetti

Contents

1. *[she sauntered from clique to clique]*

The Cheerful Scapegoat

Crocus was the first to appear at the party. She wore a dress designed by Adolph Gottlieb—a frock checkered with pictographs. Within its antic designs, she'd seek cognitive replenishment. And yet her doctor had warned, "Don't turn to inanimate patterns for emotional gratification." Thus Crocus had decided to break her monastic vow and attend the party.

Crocus, upon entering the townhouse, hid in the vestibule. She studied the pictographs on her dress. Would these conical, intersecting shapes provide a road map for the evening? Would circles and Xs and arrows, arranged with a glee practically catatonic in its excess, decode the arcane niceties of her fellow partygoers? Crocus cowered beside umbrellas and overcoats in the dim vestibule, a pathway to a party that her doctor (whom she categorized as a "miscreant-confessor") had aggressively urged her to attend.

"I won't enter the party," thought Crocus. "I will telephone my miscreant-confessor. Certainly he will give me advice."

What happened to Crocus's good cheer? Wasn't she still fantasizing about summers by the lake—humid idylls from someone else's childhood, not her own?

We will skip over the rest of the party. Other narrative duties await us, and Crocus has grown unappealing as a focus of dismay. Our dismay, an ermined entity, needs larger sway than Crocus can provide.

Suddenly remorseful for having abandoned Crocus in the vestibule, we return to her plight and decide to pose as the telephoned miscreant-confessor, to whom Crocus had placed, just a moment ago, a call intercepted by this ham-fisted voice we currently occupy, lacking another voice to articulate the distance between abstraction and figuration in the war-game rooms where decisions about nuclear eventualities are broached and bartered.

A half-hour of animated conversation commenced, on a cell phone, between the miscreant-confessor and Crocus, who took shelter in phrases that we, posing, dispensed. The miscreant-confessor then vanished, and Crocus made short work of the party. Newly bold in her Adolph Gottlieb dress, she sauntered from clique to clique.

"Do you want to see the host's bedroom?" asked a fashionable mortician whom Crocus had befriended. Crocus took the mortician's hand, and the two friends walked down a hallway to a door left ajar. Pushing open the door, Crocus walked toward the bed. The mortician refused to follow Crocus into the room; the mortician had a narrowness of viewpoint considered a sine qua non of artistic skill in earlier centuries, though her tendency to truncate every vista into a still life deprived her of the boldness required to be an effective companion and chaperone of Crocus, whose lability and chromophobia placed her in pickle after pickle, a "domino effect" of faux pas, from which she would need to be extricated by a companion exclusively committed to Crocus's weal.

Deprived of chaperone, Crocus stood over the bed, where a woman was lying on top of a man. Both were mostly clothed, though there were significant absences of habiliment, patches of disorganized skin showing through shirt-flap and pajama-fissure. The woman, who had, a moment ago, draped her body on top of the man, raised herself and stood beside Crocus. Together, this woman and Crocus looked down at the man, who remained face up; something unformed and infantile about his features provoked, in Crocus, a spasm of revulsion, as if she were looking at a Chardin painting for the first time and were not comprehending her ecstasy—a conundrum which forced Crocus to shove her rapture into a different medicine-cabinet, a hiding-place christened "Disgust."

"I've finished blowing him," said the woman to Crocus, "and now he's virtually lifeless, a passive slob, dreaming of unsolvable equations."

"Do you regret blowing him?" asked Crocus, newly enamored of this woman, because of her suave way of jettisoning responsibility for the man whom she had blown.

"I don't yet know you," said the woman, whose name, Crocus would momentarily learn, was Jesse, "but something neutral and flat in your demeanor suggests that we might together form an army."

"An army of two?" asked Crocus, already tired of being relegated to the position of meek questioner.

"I have other soldiers at my disposal," said Jesse, enigmatically brushing the hair away from her sweaty forehead.

The man on the bed woke from his stupor, and said, "Jesse, introduce me to your new friend."

"I don't yet know her name, though she seems to know mine," said Jesse.

"Crocus," volunteered the newest member of this bedroom's army.

"Pleased to meet you, Crocus," said the man on the bed, whom we will nominate as the miscreant-confessor in a new, prone, blown guise.

The hall-of-mirrors sensation overwhelmed Crocus again, as she tried to sort out the dramatis personae in the bedroom. "Am I a judge?" wondered Crocus. "Or am I a colonel in a tiny militia? Or am I simply a partygoer who stumbled into the wrong room, and should quickly exit, before I lose control of myself?"

The party's host barged in. "Hello, friends! What rebel convocation are you spoilsports forming, behind my back?"

Many years ago, before the political catastrophe that now threatened the nation, Crocus had loved the host, a tomboy named Taddeo. Once a Theodora, later a Tad, and finally a Taddeo, the host survived on the hefty earnings that came to her through sacrificial channels, sub-legal, sub-rosa, sub-material. The sub-materiality of Taddeo's sacrifices—rituals that harmed only the spirit but left unmolested the body—accrued interest through clandestine and reputedly aqueous transactions, which gave her the resources to throw legendary parties, each of them featuring a new sacrifice.

Crocus, of course, was this party's secret sacrifice. Crocus knew it, everyone knew it. Only the miscreant-confessor did not know, and that ignorance is why the miscreant-confessor dimwittedly forced Crocus to attend the party. So sectarian and convoluted were the workings of Crocus's destiny, we are surprised that she had enough pluckiness and composure to put on the Adolph Gottlieb dress without ripping it in the process of pulling the too-tight sheath over her head and attempting to slither the uncomfortable rayon over a body that no longer wished to accommodate a dead artist's pictographs.

"And now it is my turn to lie down on the foul bed," said Crocus.

"No," said Taddeo. "The sacrifice that pertains to you is happening later tonight, in the music room."

"Beside the harpsichord?" asked Crocus. Who in this metropolis did *not* know about the notorious harpsichord of Taddeo MacRae?

"Are you afraid of my harpsichord?" asked Taddeo.

"Of course Crocus is," grumbled Jesse. "Fool she'd be, not to fear an instrument designed to tangle up the minds of everyone within hearing range."

The amorphous and unnamed man on the bed, whom many in the army had typecast as the enemy, was in fact a distant descendant of Chardin. The refinement of the keen-eyed ancestor had trickled down to the man on the bed, who saw the situation around him with a lucidity that permitted him to realize that all perspective lines converged on the cone-like consciousness of Crocus. The man on the bed wiped his mouth, to free his powers of articulation from the imaginary impediment that slobber represented to a paranoid orgiast.

"Tomorrow night," Crocus said, "I fly to Nice."

"No," said the man on the bed. "No," said Taddeo. "No," said Jesse. Each "no" sounded rehearsed; the pitch of each negation was eschatologically precise, without tremor.

Instantly, Crocus gave up her plans to walk down the Promenade des Anglais. She gave up her plans to take movement classes at the hotel. She would find a movement studio here in town. She would begin movement classes the next day, if she survived the party, if the still unscripted events, destined to take place that night around the harpsichord, left her sufficiently unscarred.

"What kinds of movements am I attempting to learn?" thought Crocus. The answer didn't matter. Most important was to *plan* to learn how to move in a new way, even if these newly baptized methods had no basis in medical or spiritual fact.

"I will begin my movement classes tomorrow morning," Crocus murmured, later that evening, as she stood beside the harpsichord—the circle of partygoers surrounding the instrument and the sacrifice. "I will learn how to move like a swan. Or like a tugboat. Or like an iguana." Taddeo and Jesse smiled at Crocus, who was a good learner.

Rameau's ornamentation posed difficulties for the harpsichordist, a local hack, who lacked knowledge of period styles. The harpsichordist's mordents were clumsy, and Crocus felt stung by their maladroitness. The harpsichordist, who could no doubt sense Crocus's dismay, placed that dismay on a distant shelf in a clavier-consciousness whose only duty, tonight, lay in the parsimoniously shaped phrase, the intrusively plangent appoggiatura, the strategically irregular trill.

To leave Crocus now, in her circle of flagellants, at the mercy of a crude harpsichordist and a thrill-hungry group of behavior-experimentalists, shows no cruelty on our part. Our sympathies lie with Crocus. We admire her cheerfulness. She brings mirth and contrast to the monochromatic, humorless rooms through which she passes, on her slow journey toward tomorrow's movement classes, taught by incompetent masters with no grasp of kinetic fundamentals, and no tenderness for the bodies whose flesh is subject to the palpations and distensions of movement-sages without scruple. We admire the movement teachers, despite their unethical haggardness. "Tomorrow I will find a new way to move," Crocus continued to murmur. The harpsichordist ignored her senseless mutterings. A good instrumentalist must pay strict attention to the tempo. Without a steady yet flexible pulse, the piece approaches ruin. Ruin might be a good goal, however, if Crocus's sufferings are to be our guide. Crocus's consciousness burned down to the slimmest filament of plausibility. And yet its flame continued to attract flagellants and admirers. Around Crocus, the admirers stayed fast within their circle formation. The admirer-flagellants held hands, to keep the circle serene and firm. Crocus began to dance—if you call those stumbling steps a dance. The movement class was already in process, and it had no teacher. "I am already where tomorrow told me I must wait for it to arrive," Crocus said, in a loud, clear voice. Her dance-collapse, a cross between resurrection and ruin, attained a new fixity and vividness. "This dance is where we must now live," she continued, in her bright confident tone. She staggered and regained balance and staggered again. The circle of flagellant-admirers clapped their hands rhythmically, with a ferocity veined by igneous strands of kindness. To call our behavior *kind*—to call this congregation *civilized*—requires an imagination addicted to the fumes that rise from notoriety. Who is notorious tonight? Crocus is newly notorious, and will remain so as long as she continues to carve out, through non-movement, a movement class without master. Now we must efface this sordid investigation by rubbing a turpentine-soaked rag over the figure's already smeared features.

The Cheerful Scapegoat in the Suburbs

The suburb where the cheerful scapegoat resided, Havoc Town, hardly lacked homoerotic resources. Near the Ferris wheel, a splendid tea room remained in operation, a well-furnished habitat where traveling salesmen could congregate, and where the cheerful scapegoat, Marty, worked as attendant. His responsibilities were few: to keep replenished the supply of toilet paper rolls; to mop the floors; to change light bulbs; to empty the trash receptacles; to serve as educator and guard, making sure that no excessively cruel activities took place.

Unlike most tea rooms, the facility adjacent to the oft-praised Ferris wheel was not kept a secret from the suburb's permanent residents. A small plaque outside the tea room memorialized its function in loving yet terse phrases: "Havoc Town is proud to host the longest-running tea room in homosexual history. Founded in 1889." The tea room saw its fortunes decline during the two world wars, but during the American "boom" years of economic and imperial expansion, the tea room received favorable notices in family periodicals, including *The Saturday Evening Post*, where columnist June Osteng described the facility as "gracious in exterior, brooding at cocktail hour, and never gauche."

Marty endured minor hardships as caretaker, despite the suburb's beneficent attitude toward the tea room. Marty sat on a stool outside the tea room from noon until 9 p.m. Any insults that came his way he took in stride, with a cheerfulness that he attributed to early dental care. To tell the truth, dentists *tout court* were absent from his childhood. What we are calling "early dental care" was in fact a steady gnawing on carrots. In Marty's adult diet, as a consequence, he downplayed crudités.

Lonely was the walk from carrotless kitchen to plush tea room, until a suburban representative arrived to perform an inspection tour of the cruising premises. The person entrusted with the labor of inspection, Wicker, tied Marty to his stool, while close study of the tea room's contours occurred. The rope dug into Marty's bare legs; he was wearing running shorts, because the weather forecast had warned of temperatures soaring to 95 degrees in the shade. Marty didn't mind the rope's chafing effect on his skin, as he waited for Wicker to peruse and remonstrate the tea room's conditions.

For the moment, we will leave Marty tied up, enduring rope injuries, however mild, while we offer the reader some brief instruction on the role of minor seconds in music. The minor second is the theater for combat between two notes of adjacent pitch. Micro-pitches and quarter-pitches cannot be considered seriously in today's discussion, unfortunately, though many of us in Havoc Town are fond of internecine terror, the internal friction that ensues when a note grows unsure of its ontological status.

"Pretty thing," said Marty, as Wicker emerged from the tea room, a satisfied smile on the inspector's face indicating a favorable outcome.

"I don't have absolute jurisdiction over this tea room," said Wicker. "Though Havoc Town owns the waterways that feed the latrines, that ownership doesn't give us the right to shut down the tea room, even if its practices disobey national regulations."

"Fritillary, fritillary," murmured Marty, happy that his inferior position gave him license to cast spells. "Fritillary" was an incantation guaranteed to rupture Wicker's calm.

"Are you homosexual?" asked Wicker. "The tea room is impeccable and grand, like a steamship. But your nature confuses me."

"The men I admit into my body are mostly strangers to Havoc Town," said Marty, "but none of these acts take place in the tea room. My contract forbids on-site sex."

"Where do you take your clients?" asked Wicker.

"To the woods," said Marty, serene in the knowledge that this response would decimate Wicker.

Let us interrupt their obscene colloquy for a moment to say another word about the minor second. In the homosexual underground of the 1920s, a minor second in music gave introspection its opportunity for riding roughshod over speakeasy codes. Do we owe you an explanation for lamplight, or can we die into it? To "die into lamplight" is a 1920s North American idiom; it means "to remain sanguine about lacerations occurring during the conversation." You *die into* the laceration committed by the other; one party in the conversation destroys the other, and the destroyed member responds not with fisticuffs but with a dying motion—not *dying* in the sense of collapsing, fainting, or lapsing into coma; but *dying* in the sense of losing distinct edges. You agree to *die into* the other conversationalist; you cede agency, meanwhile polishing the silver slipcase of your own inner tabernacle.

"Tabernacle, nuncle," said Marty, privy to every nuance. No need for Marty to explain "tabernacle" to Wicker, even though Wicker had little knowledge of religious traditions other than his own sect's blasphemous practices.

"The nacre of my tabernacle," said Marty, as Wicker undid the ropes.

"Here, in a suburb?" asked Wicker.

All authoritative personages in Havoc Town nursed an obsequious terror of being identified as suburban, and yet they threw around the word *suburb* as freely as frankincense, to fumigate any conversation and make it navigable.

The next day, Wicker and Marty met for a drink at the Venus Institute, a bar on the desolate highway outside Havoc Town, whose purchase on the name *suburb* was meager, because no dominating city lay near.

Either Wicker or Marty would need to die by the end of the night. This realization dawned on each of the men simultaneously. Only Marty, however, because of his cheerfulness, had the wit to develop a plan of action that would lead to this prophecy's fulfillment.

The murder weapon would be a winch, Marty decided. The murder would be justified by the sacredness of the tea room over which he held watch. The suburban elders would forgive the crime, because the victim had elected himself inspector without having been hired to perform the job, and these acts of hubristic self-advancement justified punishment, however ultimate. Havoc Town didn't outlaw severe punishments, as long as they were meted out with merciful quickness.

What had Wicker done wrong? He had not penetrated Marty. He had merely tied Marty up while performing an inspection of a tea room whose historic status demanded constant verification, lest the tea room slide into a decrepitude that rubbed against its noble reputation, as two notes in a minor second rub against each other to create havoc.

"My foreskin aches," said Marty, with a solemnity befitting a layperson offering extreme unction to a snotty passerby. "The tense relations within our suburb have lodged in my organs. The frenum is where I experience suburban rancor and rivalry most keenly."

"If I were to touch your frenum now, would the foreskin stop aching?" asked Wicker, as if subliminally aware that his own execution was a foregone conclusion.

"I don't supervise the tea room," said Marty. "I simply clean it."

"You do a good job cleaning it," said Wicker.

"I don't participate in the action," said Marty. "As a mini-dictator of the action, I'm nearby and dominant, but never directly soiled or aroused."

Their discourse's abstraction was leavened by the arrival of a third round of dry martinis.

One exigency now clouded Marty's mind: winch-procurement. Where to find a winch in a suburb encircled by a lonely highway with no roadside attractions?

To stand above Marty and be his confessor is no small pleasure; such satisfactions only come to those, like us, who inspect the inspector, who have the prerogative of murdering any inspector whose conduct lacks punctiliousness.

Our nature, as inspector of the inspector, goes unexamined, and thus grows prone to filth. Confidently we may assert that our nature, supra-suburban—that is, *lording it over the suburbs as a tyrant over a serf*—need not ride the Ferris wheel of your fitful regard, but may claim the power to decimate you, as well. Our powers, limitless, suggest that we might eventually run for public office.

Marty could find no winch, and so he brought Wicker back home to the apartment that Marty rented in the valley below Havoc Town, a valley less noble than the suburb that loomed above it, a valley that, despite its relative worthlessness, still was a legal part of Havoc Town and enjoyed the privileges that come with complete surrender to a superior municipality. That night, Marty and Wicker engaged in arcane forms of intercourse; Marty's bodily sensations were heightened by memories of being-inspected, and by half-formed fantasies of fritillaries and winches that never had the kindness to materialize when they were needed.

Where, within this fable, may Marty rest his head and sleep? Or must Marty remain imprisoned by what one fawning local novelist has called "the watches of the night"? Must Marty supervise the fable, lest the fable murder him while he is sleeping?

Marty woke up at five in the morning—a slumber broken by alcoholic excess. Wicker lay snoring in bed, next to Marty, who sat up, disgusted by the proximity of an inspector.

Quickly Marty ransacked the apartment, and found, in a rarely opened cabinet, a serviceable winch. The winch made noise as it performed the work that only a winch can do, but Wicker never regained consciousness; Wicker's transition from sleep to death was seamless. Marty supervised the transition; he inspected each instant of the transition, to make sure that the passageway was justified. Only a perfectly logical and morally sound transport between sleep and death could allay the anxieties of a tea room attendant nervous about job stability and about his own place in a cosmology spinning out of a benign deity's control.

Dispensing with Wicker's body, a straightforward task, filled Marty with no melancholy. By noon, he could return, rested and not unduly perplexed, to his position outside the tea room. Two teenagers accosted Marty, later that afternoon, and pounded his skull against the pavement, because Marty had a reputation for surrendering easily to mortification, and the teenagers were curious about the transition between supervision and death.

The Cheerful Scapegoat (We Three)

You published a new book, *Transplantations Medical*. We discussed the odd title. The word "transplantations" recalled your painful emigration to this country, and the plantations shadowing our immoral nation's history. *Transplantations Medical*, like *Paradise Lost*, put the noun before the adjective. "The lost paradise of the medical transplantation," I suggested, fixing the inversion—but already you were angry and confused.

You'd suffered medical injuries, wounds I was incapable of discussing with sufficient empathy; and so you urged me to discontinue the conversation.

I persisted. I wanted to discuss transsexual existences. Everything I'd ever felt or seen could fall under the category of "transsexual"—but then the classification system, which had promised momentarily to comprehend me, faltered, if a system can falter...

On top of the hill a new rest home opened. Different existences, stacked on top of each other—or do I mean "different bodies"?—opened to my curious fingers. "A home can't open to fingers," I said, hoping that you would pull all copies of *Transplantations Medical* from the shelves, and rewrite the book, and include a new chapter, discussing my fingers and their preternatural capacity to open new rest homes on hilltops.

You and I drove to the waterfront. One texture rose to the fore—a nubbiness I couldn't explain. I sank away from the possibility of explanation, and tried instead to touch your summer jacket's cottony protuberances.

You'd dedicated *Transplantations Medical* to me—a benediction I didn't deserve, though it enlarged my sway. Because you were a best-selling writer translated into twenty-four languages, readers around the globe would discover me, ponder my existence, fantasize about my body. Clever interpreters would understand that my physique's peculiarity, which shall go undescribed, was one of the transplantations cited in the title.

You masturbated, then, in front of me, as we sat on a bench overlooking the harbor. Perhaps you weren't masturbating; perhaps you were simply lodging a complaint against yourself, and the complaint took the form of finger-play. I turned away, to give you privacy; I considered returning to the bar and ordering a lobster roll. We could split the roll, after you had finished your distracting episode of self-stimulation—whether a hobby or a livelihood, I couldn't discern.

You weren't nude, though you were investigating your body with repeated, subtle motions. I alternated between watching your investigation and watching what passed for "activity" on the bay. This activity consisted of three night-crawling boats, small and perhaps not navigated by humans. The boats were evenly spaced, never overlapping, but the middle boat seemed to wish to speed ahead of the others.

"Fellow animals," said a man, startling us. "May I share this bench of happenstance with you?" He urged his body between ours. We made way for him, and let his corpulence bisect our comity.

"Slate," you said. "Dear Slate." You embraced him. You'd met in the hospital, after your trolley accident. Slate had been visiting his sister, who was also a patient in the emergency room. He befriended you, returned to see you every day of your hospitalization, watched your swellings subside and your contusions heal. As you recovered, a romance blossomed, watered by pity.

On Slate's nose, a flap of skin seemed ready to disengage, as if he, too, had been subject to transplantations. I felt an impulse to tug at the flap, to complete its process of lazy migration away from the nose proper.

You noticed the flap and tore it off. Slate screamed, and then laughed. "Good riddance," he said. "I'd meant to ask a dermatologist to complete the refiguration."

"Last call for lobster rolls," I said. I offered to buy one for us to share; I would ask the bartender to split it into equal portions.

The bartender told me that she was out of lobster. Would pike suffice? She cut the roll into thirds.

"Pike," said Slate, when I explained the substitution, "takes me back to childhood, before I was what you suburban clods call a 'bum.' In the summer, Dad and I would go fishing. We'd drive to the bridge, and cast our poles over the edge. Then a superhighway project came along, and the community didn't put up a fight. Fishing opportunities dwindled. Dad lost his job at the accounting firm, started drinking, grew violent. I began turning tricks, as revenge. Dad wanted me to save myself for marriage. Wedlock, I believed, was rot—a pious sewage system. I had no intention of corralling myself into dead arrangements. I flouted Dad and the law, but the law pursued me. Three years in prison—and then, a hardscrabble life on the streets. Slowly I climbed back to bookishness."

You turned to me and explained, "In the emergency room, Slate kept vigil over my bed."

"And when you got out of the hospital," Slate continued, "I helped you with manual composition. I didn't mind not being credited as co-author. I contributed only a few paragraphs per chapter."

I watched the three boats on the bay. They were approaching the lighthouse, its signal pulsating, as if issuing a decree. Who could figure out whether the signal was hopeful or pessimistic?

I wanted desperately to be included in the story Slate was telling about your relationship's sordid prehistory, but I also feared the consequences of Slate discovering that you had dedicated *Transplantations Medical* to me. I was a good enough judge of character to intuit that Slate might be willing to maim me as punishment for stealing the limelight.

The three of us woke the next morning in your bed: a car alarm, on the street, ruptured our sleep. In the middle of the night, we'd each suffered food poisoning, a mild case, not so dire that it interfered with our nascent, tripartite intimacy. One by one we'd risen from bed to do our business in the lavatory—then back to sleep for a few dehydrated hours.

That afternoon we visited the new rest home on the hill. Preliminary research, you said, in preparation for your next book, the sequel to *Transplantations Medical*. Cognitive enfeeblement would be the new volume's subject.

Slate agreed to take a job at the rest home, as mole, to do undercover research. I volunteered to write empirical paragraphs, to bolster your book's grasp on the veritable. Facts came easily to me. You specialized in ghosts, predictions, epiphenomena. Your authority in matters figmental spread your reputation around the globe. Buried within the speculations were the facts I subserviently pilfered for your sake, from sources as various as park benches and harbor vistas.

One morning, late in the sequel's composition, I looked deeply into Slate's eyes. No trace of the nose refiguration remained visible. Slate's nose was large, but only in profile. As I stared into his eyes, his nose seemed to diminish in size and importance. My sexual relationship with Slate had intensified; your body had never appealed to me, and as the cognitive enfeeblement project evolved, your impoverished imagination and remorseless judgments soured me on the prospect of ever embracing you again. I would consent to sit beside you while you investigated your own body with strange half-indiscernible movements of wrist and fingers, but I wouldn't participate. Into Slate's eyes, however, I could contentedly gaze with a sense of nostalgia for the father who didn't approve of Slate's early career as hustler. The "Dad" of Slate's narration grew more palpable to me, as Slate held me in his rough arms. The "Dad" of Slate's narration, no longer a weekend fisherman, no longer a son-bruiser, now only a suggestion of flannel shirts and flexed dorsal muscles, thickened into more than figment, as I surrendered to Slate's caresses. You would not have called it surrender. You, more intellectually adept, would have found a frostier word. I would like you to describe Slate's attachment to my body, his style of making my body his own. How would you depict the regularity or fitfulness of his thrusts, shoves, and adhesions?

Slate claimed amnesia. "I blacked out," he said. "I lost track of my hands. Was I touching you, or touching myself? Or were my hands not involved in our lonely yet overpopulated congress?"

Occasional opened windows in the rest home admitted nearby sounds of revelers, with their guitars, tambourines, cymbals, and kettle-drums. From the hill, one could look down upon the town and the harbor. The revelers arrived and departed without a schedule; whenever I had the good fortune of visiting Slate in the rest home, while he was engaged in undercover research, I savored the unannounced sounds of mallets striking drum-skins. Would you include these sounds in your sequel? I will ask you tonight. I wish I could claim loyalty to a cause ethically keener than your sequel or those unseen drums—but Slate has quashed my idealism. The scar on his stomach—a knife-wound he won't explain—remains red and raised. You could make it vanish if you were omnipotent, but you suffer, as do I, from truncated vision. Shake-clatter-shake went the tambourine outside the rest-home window as Slate kissed me, a kiss that would, I hope, undo my subservience to sound and to sequel.

Slate's phallus unnaturally tapered at its head. That was not my favorite genital configuration. I told him so. You felt otherwise. You savored the pointy kind. You called it "rare, not porcine." To it—the pointiness—I applied my usual straightforwardness. I handled it, the end and the beginning, with a docility almost ductile in its willingness to stay away from the higher frequencies of rage. To the whims of Slate's pointiness I cheerfully hearkened, with hand and mouth and any other aspect of my physique that I could muster. My capacities for mustering were limited, fabulously so. You indicted me for these limitations, and, later, wrote about the indictment. Again and again you and I would sit on the harbor bench and discuss my limitations.

2. *[your dormant orifices]*

Pulling Lashes

The boy pulled his lashes because Barbra Streisand told him to pull them. She wanted his vocal prowess—meager—to fall apart. She was tired of being the center of attention in the women's bathroom, where Eve Arden and company had long ago gathered, against the boy's will; the boy objected to Eve Arden, as he objected to everything coral, everything not fixed. He wanted to pull out his eyelashes because they intruded—he yearned to differentiate horizontals from verticals, and to overcome the orange semi-circle that was his chair as well as his soap opera. He couldn't communicate his distress to Streisand. The two were facing in opposite directions, as Dorian Gray always faced away from Andy Warhol, or Willa Cather away from Karl Marx. Can you explain the oppositional defiant disorder afflicting Streisand and Cather, Marx and Fanny Brice? "Your elbow presses too firmly into the blue table," said Eve Arden, before our boy-protagonist was born; he overheard her whispers when he pressed his ear against the damaged, porous shell of lost time, like pressing against the thin wall separating two bedrooms on the MGM set where he auditioned for the death scene in *Dorian Gray* (the climax, when the *débauché* surrenders his autonomy and bequeaths it to a work of art). Barbra and the boy-man figurine were talking about tessitura and portamento, how to slide out of your identity into the nearby semblance of red coral—a Murano glass sculpture—resting on a table whose blueness husbanded its own impossibilities, nasal and vaguely labial.

Gardener's Scarf

Fruitlessly you wait for the gardener to show up on the red bench where he has promised to meet you after his shift ends. You encountered him in the bathroom at the museum, and you followed him back to his botanical garden, crowded with statuary and obelisks, a thick-enough assortment to make Peggy Guggenheim jealous, if she were alive and peering now through a window at you, who refuse to reciprocate her gaze. Avoidance tactics doom you and determine your fall from competence into a gutter clogged with torn back-issues of *ONE*. The sculptures in the garden have more solidity—more conviviality—than you do, faded ash-blond melancholy man under a sky too pink for its own good, the pink of a wrestling match held in the white palace on the hill, a *Women in Love* villa, where Oliver Reed and Alan Bates will strip, and you will not suffer the children to enter Ken Russell's kingdom of horniness and assuagements. (Or do I mean *asides?*) I will seize your assets if you seize mine. The bench is crooked and you despise your own immobility; I speak on your behalf because I am a Sally, a male Sally, or a transmuting Sally without a specific destination on the gender spectrum. Infantine, I stared and stared at the ecclesiastical gardener you too await, the gardener you met in the bathroom at the Byzantine museum—or am I that stranger, too? Your sad-sack retrievals cannot equal the distaste that the no-show gardener feels for your face, so meretriciously and deceptively young you can't grow a beard. Green is an underrated color—it can include viridian and grass and jade and ocean and tiredness and a near-death experience at 4 p.m. in a nether city shaped like one or two or three of your dormant orifices.

That Odd Summer of '84

I wore pajamas as outerwear—in public—and became like Heidegger or Freud, wanting to speed up history while getting credit for slowing it down. My friend was in a bad car accident; he recovered, and in his new, mended body he joined me by the felicitous river. He held a hammer and I was in danger. I kept on becoming transsexual without intending to. The forest of feathers and serrations (like bread knives) surrounding us was an invitation Antigone might have complained about; I sank into the puce possibility of joining Persephone at the nail salon, where we could sit around and eat "failure chips," a new sage-and-lavender-scented snack, a feast rude and divagating as my masculine friend's indigo-jeans-clad knee, its hunkiness too late for me to embrace. I could sink into how political I was in 1984, sink back into the lumpy chin and Adam's apple I had in those post-Watergate days, when I was more girl than boy, or more apple than rotunda—I mean the Villa La Rotonda, a joke by Palladio, my boyfriend and I sitting under its cupola and waiting for a jagged-mouthed philosopher (Pascal or Merleau-Ponty) to become not so obvious in his retributive lust for me, the kind of lust that makes you want to destroy the desired object. This ghost-philosopher in the corner wasn't the main conversation piece; "boyfriend" and "I" were the tryst's shamed stars. But the philosopher kept rising up from the flora and fauna to analyze the confetti striations of my friend's reluctance to spit enough on my genitals to make the operation smooth and mutually pleasurable.

Sorting Out Andy

The possessions couldn't move forward, and his butt on the cane chair hovered, hoping to avoid landing. Hoarder, Andy wanted cake more than he wanted the Greek terpsichorean mask that would undo him if he let its blank eyes in on the secret. Each of the surfaces offered a reward, but none of the satisfactions could equal the walnut he became by wishing himself five years old again, a runt cutting out a flower from a steel can, listening to the Victrola, measuring his nose, invalidating Beethoven, paging through the telephone book so he could find a woman listener named Betty Begonia. He would call up Betty and pretend to be her long-lost sister. And you, too, though not a prank caller by avocation, would be punished for letting the rug slide to a different position on the floor. You would shout at your father for insisting that the rug remain in its legislated place, the nuclear war position; you wanted the rug to occupy instead a "gay deceivers" latitude, or a "hidden persuaders" longitude, like ads with naked eighteen-year-old male hustlers, propagandistic inducements hidden near Campbell's soup cans. You wanted to buy beef consommé, because the treasure trail leading down from your persecutor's navel into unbuttoned Levi's promised to elevate your life or erase it. And then I intervened, wearing a leather bib. She told me to close my eyes—Andy's mother did—and said I would thereby find a tiddlywinks nirvana, a faux-Tiepolo cumulus ceiling. Space, Andy decided, could be flattened through the decisive censoring action of a murmured whim—*Goodbye volume, goodbye perspective, goodbye modeling, goodbye crosshatching, goodbye depth.* I tried to take off Andy's pants, and that attempt was part of what Andy's mother called my "autism," by which she meant my shutterbug addiction to carnival. I would end up training my camera on his mother, too—I understood how casually and whimsically she wanted to destroy herself as a way of making the Fiestaware less depressing. Did she admire the impossible teal contrapposto of a boy-torso tracing its melancholy in the grisaille of a muumuu-clad Apollo, a varicose-veined gymnast I could undress with my X-ray glasses? Could we revive *My Fair Lady* soon? Andy's mother was graceful when she slapped me. And on the rug I fell, facedown, writhing with closure.

Bloomsbury Revisited

My highly patterned languor was not an invitation for you to destroy or despoil me. Nor did Schiele hold a grudge against Job. Nor did Matisse fall in love with Sappho. The roughly delineated marks of your regard for me led us back to that ditch beside the elementary school—the Bloomsbury Preparatory Academy, if you insist—where a dead body was once discovered. Who deposited the corpse in that bamboo grotto, that patch of malfeasance on Graves Drive, near Alfred Mews, across the moat from Arizona? I had plans to punish the other children, to turn them into dandies by taking away their dignity; with a perfume atomizer I sprayed my disregard onto their pusillanimous faces, those little boys and girls and in-betweens who hypothesized a dead body in that ditch so they could pile their love of oceans on top of the rumored remains. Perhaps a newspaper announcing the end of the Great War covered the dead limbs in that school-abutting ditch; or perhaps the movie *Wings*, with its gay romance, first Academy Award-winning Best Picture, undid my identification with the corpse? In any case, at the Burbank Theater, near Bloomsbury's toxic edge, I visited the half-lit restroom to make friends with the cineastes and buggers, and to turn my love of pattern into a body part as despised and lionized as Van Gogh's ear, propped on a toilet tank to attract a loitering Salome. On a blue bench dwarfed by overgrown pyrachantha in the cruisy park I sat, waiting for my drug deal to materialize, because my father told me to write a fairy tale based on Rumpelstiltskin but didn't tell me the plot, so I had to invent a *Cities of the Plain* reconceptualization of Rumpelstiltskin, dripping with the varieties of ambiguous fluids that fall from the undisclosed parts of the sodomized populations, grateful for their fixes, like fine-etched veins in a red-figure vase that will guide you to the high school prom to greet Medusa's mother, the moonlight a permissive chaperone, authorizing the high school partygoers to drink vodka and then vomit in the Klimt bushes.

3. *[the remorse plague]*

Green Ice Cream Man I Didn't Love

The man was green, but the ice cream he sold, from his corner truck, wasn't green. He didn't carry pistachio or mint.

The ice cream man I didn't love seemed to be floating in green ether—or seemed to have been born from a green womb. The womb's greenness clung to him for the rest of his life. His penis was particularly green, he told me, when we hugged, behind his ice cream truck. The ice cream man I didn't love was always eager to hug me, because, he said, "You look like a movie star." I'm not glamorous. Pasty, scrawny, I have a large scar on my forehead.

I touched the butt of the ice cream man I didn't love. I touched his butt during one of our protracted hugs, behind his ice cream truck. His butt, lazy, harbored no remorse. Nor should a mere pair of buttocks feel contrite. Why is it the business of buttocks to huddle down with the emotions? Why must turbid anxieties disturb the calm of buttocks whose only ambition is to remain affixed to the legs and hips and torso of a person trying to make a living?

My sadism and remorselessness—almost equal to the remorselessness of Edgardo's buttocks—will eventually doom me to become as green as Edgardo. Only in the last paragraph of this little narrative have I chosen to reveal the protagonist's name. I waited to tell you his name because I am afraid that Edgardo's family will read this tale and sue me for disclosing sordid details about their green paterfamilias. We are grateful that no one will ever read this tale, and that no one will contact Edgardo's family. We are grateful to be invisible, not yet green, though eventually Edgardo's greenness will become my own.

And Then I Threw My Hands in the Air

"And then I threw my hands in the air. My camisole had turned yellow, a sea-change. Had the gas begun to penetrate my lungs and blood vessels? Was my incompetence in the process of being discovered by the nation's surveillance system? That's a good one, I chuckled. My face essentially folded in half, in a hospitality basement—that is, in the basement of a hotel famed for forgetfulness. The maenad in me—I called the maenad 'John Donne'—had become the equivalent of Freud's 'secondary process,' and as a result I was lying in a meadow of heather, my face buried nonstop (like Cassandra's) in the cat-gut strings of the blooms, which make me laugh and sneeze and whistle and issue directives, totalitarian dictations. To coincide with a phenomenon, rather than to glimpse it from outside! I haven't spoken to them in three hours—the surveillance committee in the hospitality basement—and I must complete my time-sheet soon. I've acquired a festering disease, lying here in a field of heather… Radical indecision, unvisualizable and finite: am I on a blooming meadow, or am I in a basement? Am I the star of a remake of *Woman in the Dunes*? Am I the director of the remake, a jazzed-up and goldenrod version of the afterwardsness original, an original film obsessed with afterwardsness, *après-coup*, like what they talk about at MIT? Everything's wonderful in the hospitality basement, where I'm hired to sweep and curry favor with traveling idiots. Basically I'm under linden trees, a contrarian under the lindens. That's final."

The Red Door

I walked through the red door because I'm in the habit of walking through red doors.

I didn't bump my head on the door. I opened it. The door rebuked me for opening it.

Accustomed to rebuke, I tried to divide into three bite-sized pieces the door's harsh verdict on my conduct.

The door didn't have a mouth, but the door spoke; it cautioned me to keep quiet about my penchant for self-division.

I'm treating the door—in this fable—as if it were a tree in *The Wizard of Oz*, a talking tree, whose boughs weigh heavily on Judy Garland as she walks beneath them.

Judy Garland, that morning, was preoccupied with her name, Gumm, her real name. The word *Gumm* moved in and out of her consciousness.

As I sit on my porch now, thinking about the red door I walked through, I can picture the word *Gumm* moving through Judy's consciousness, the surname moving with a peculiar undulation of the hips, if a mere word can have hips.

On this porch, where I await the verdict from the oncologist, I rock back and forth on a black-and-red rocking chair my feeble agèd aunt gave me the year before she died. Her death and the rocking chair have much in common. Red enamel details on the chair protrude from the black wood as vividly as my aunt's teeth protruded from her gums as she lay in her hospital bed. Doing my death-bed vigil duties, I stared at her gums and tried to find them beautiful. I owed it to my aunt to make one aspect of her death a thing of beauty, as Keats once wrote, lying.

Keats distorted the evidence. So did Victor Fleming, director of *The Wizard of Oz*. The phlegm in Fleming—unfortunate name—prevented me from imagining that he treated Judy with kid gloves, though I wanted to imagine that he was kind to Judy. I wanted to imagine that Victor Fleming didn't criticize her body, her posture, her appetites.

I walked through the red door because I wanted the critics to stop rebuking me for my appetites. Who are these critics, pray tell? Do these critics exist? Or are they merely juridical phantoms I've cooked up to alleviate my gout?

Christ on the cross, like me walking through the red door, needed to fit his pain into a small space. Everyone watched Christ squeeze himself into his moment of crucifixion. I walked through the red door without the benefit of a chorus of witnesses. If I'm doomed to suffer, I want no one to watch my suffering, no one to turn my agony into a TV series.

Can I explain one more thing to you, or is it already your bedtime?

I bit into a caraway rye roll this morning and pretended it was Judy Garland's talent. My bite was a love-bite, gentle, aimed toward digestion and praise.

Above the red door was an explanatory lintel, on which I saw inscribed the tell-tale phrase, *Broadway Melody of 1938*. When I encountered those words, for the first time, I didn't understand them. Only later—only now—do I see the resemblance of *Broadway Melody of 1938* to bedsheets soaked by night sweats.

The Terror of Complications

Maybe I mean the *terroir* of complications—a certain flinty vineyard in Chablis, where complicated tastes abound?

At the hospital, I saw the nurse bring the newborn infant into the mother's room. I had no legitimate function in the room. I wasn't the father. I wasn't even a close friend of the mother. I was a reporter from the *Times*, but which *Times*?

The mother lifted the baby. To her breast the mother affixed the baby, in a moment of compassion and spite. The baby began to familiarize itself with the offered nipple. The baby was instinctively drawn to the nipple but also tentative in seizing it. The mother herself was just a kid, not willing to take on the dreadful responsibility of feeding this scrap of an infant, this poor excuse for a human being.

Inside my chest I felt a cough begin to form itself: a small lump of contagion. The lump had threads attached to it, and I was responsible for each of the threads, like telephone wires. The movement of the contagion-lump, in my chest—the lump's palpitations—resembled an earthquake coming to consciousness, for the first time, of its potential to destroy Crete.

Let me backtrack. The mother's name was Florence James. The infant's name was Titian James. Titian had a red birthmark on its neck. Florence, seeing the birthmark, felt cough-like threads form in her heart—swirling tendrils she wanted to extirpate. Florence James decided, "I will refine my consciousness through elaborate yet unseen acts of masochism, and through these refinements I will destroy the spider-web filaments that tie my incipient croup to Titian's birthmark— the red mark marring the neck of my first-born, a child I plan to disavow after I leave this hospital."

Florence continued, "The color of the tendrils—connecting my nascent cough to Titian's birthmark—is ochre, or copper, if copper had been smashed in the head or lightly swatted and thereby turned into a harmless, unlovable iridescence."

You can see that I feel great responsibility for Florence's consciousness. You can also probably discern that I feel no empathy for Titian. Titian doesn't belong to the realm of art. Titian is a mistake. In his capacity as mistake I nominate him for a position on Golgotha. I am a reporter for the *Golgotha Times*, the newspaper of record for a little-known nation-state, the Kingdom of Needless Suffering.

Telephone Receivers or Cooking Spoons in Purple Haze

"The big lesson I learned from my year of immersion in purple emulsion—a viscous medium used for cloning—was how to quell anxiety in Botticelli admirers, those steely-gazed lemmings who bring their salty provisions in paper sacks to the Uffizi and stand around waiting for analog revelation. It's better to be lascivious at home, to pluck my eyebrows and apply Anusol to my itchy areas, those cavities sparse in pity and rife with nerve endings. Right? Like a Bauhaus craphole? A Tenderloin technology will soon be invented to recreate homosexual utopias in the desert, like Marfa: new choreographies, new vulgarities. Brian Eno and the Supremes formed a threaded-together "you" and "you," an *après-coup*, an afterwardsness I was doomed to reconstruct because I'd forfeited the original fire; the original flame walked by on high heels, an apparition I couldn't drink or transform into vaudeville. What were the words I'd spun? Please don't start talking about Botticelli again. An elevated drawing of Fallopian tubes—was that the original flame I'd lost in the desert? Or was it a one-point perspective drawing of Fallopian tubes, seen from Botticelli's point of view? And was the much-mourned afterwardsness just a sandwich of litterbug potentialities, a swizzle-stick Lady

Bird Johnson plaint intoned like the terrible Stock Market crash of 1904, when the futures of anyone worth mentioning grew unappetizing as a pizza—a pizza I'm trying to reconstruct (it's the pizza I call "the original fire")? On that pizza, small triangles of an unnameable substance were nestled amid the cheese. And I was impatient—impatient as an avocado, the most unsteady fruit, always waiting to ripen, never ripening. And as I wait, avocado-like, to ripen, I try to remember the name of the fruit that preceded me, the fruit I incarnated before I became avocado-like, before the Stock Market crash of 1904. I picked up the telephone in 1904 even though the telephone I picked up was a princess receiver that hadn't yet been invented. And on that princess phone I heard the message from the desert I'm trying to reconstruct now—a message warning me about pointe shoes, about the torture of trying to fit your soul's motility into claustrophobia-inducing forms. Something else I'd tried to communicate to you, in that lost epoch—something about purple itself, its power to make everything a hazard, a toss of the dice… What else did I hide in that secret briefcase now buried under the sands? Had I locked in that briefcase some notes about the remorse plague that spread from mouth to mouth? The remorse I'm trying to describe and remember—it too was a triangle, like the substance nestled into the cheese on the forgotten pizza. The triangle was a small tucked-in object, a proclivity more than a personage. I set sail for that refinement, that edge of a proclivity, on whose shore I would one day land, my boat in tatters. I can't end this complaint until I remember every detail of what happened in the desert asylum that summer, a drugged confinement I fallaciously bless with the name *afterwardsness* just because that word erupted in the middle of a Supremes tune never sung but held out as a promise of future reward. I could grow a very long beard and put ice in a tall glass and wait for that reward. Or I could return to the memory of that salmon bun I've been trying to reconstruct, a bun whose dough was pink and yellow—yellow from polenta, and pink from the flecks of dried salmon the careless cook had tossed into the flour. I'm not mocking the salmon bun by mentioning it. I'm begging you to take the salmon bun seriously, and to sing about it to your children. If you ever have children. If the remorse contagion doesn't strike you down first. How water can flow over the thought of the salmon bun but never destroy the bun and never destroy the thought itself, the thought that holds the salmon bun like a salty potentiality, perishable and not freaked out!"

4. *[a chemistry set suitable for toddlers]*

The Snow Falls On…

If I knew what the snow fell on, I could triumph over the current political regime, which has its own perverse style of landing on surfaces; this regime falls on my body with the ambiguous force of a milkshake spilling on a diner floor.

I am not a milkshake, so I don't have the power to spill; I can collaborate with milkshakes by drinking them or making them, but I can't incarnate a milkshake.

Sheila, however, knew how. Sheila tried to teach me. She said, "Imitate my dance steps. Their ambient felicities, like a transparent tango skirt, will offer you a pornotopic vista." If I were not standing so close to Sheila, in a dance studio on West 15th Street, I could avoid the cluster headache embodied in the word *pornotopic*. But I am a mere three inches away from Sheila, and I have already fallen under her spell.

Sheila is a dancer I offended, long ago, by spending too many entranced hours staring at the shadow she cast on the boardwalk. I stooped to the seaside pavement, and with pale blue chalk I traced her silhouette, as she stood, lording it over me, in a tango skirt that wasn't transparent.

The power relations between Sheila and me oscillate. Their non-fixity is a heavy snowfall landing right now on a tame Rottweiler wearing a fancy alpaca snow-shield, to protect the Rottweiler, a pacifist, from catching pneumonia. Dogs can catch pneumonia. Dogs can be pacifists. Dogs can be fashion plates. Dogs can be wayfarers in snowy Flemish landscapes. I can't be a dog, however, just as I can't be a milkshake, and just as I can't avoid the instructions Sheila is now giving me: "dance, dance, dance." If I had a draft card, I'd burn it. If Sheila could forge me a draft card, I'd thank her, and then I'd burn it. I speak to you as paid representative of Sheila's dance studio, which doesn't yet rule the land.

Pincushion with Thimble

Cress chatted. Could I become Cress, quickly, by wearing a reindeer sweater? To whom was Cress chatting? Why was I suddenly at war with Cress?

Cress—short for Cressida—rented an apartment next to mine. Through thin walls, I could hear Cress chatting all night. Presumably, these were phone conversations; I couldn't hear the voice of her interlocutor—only Cress's voice, filling the air with unnecessary racket.

I was playing the lead in a local *Bye Bye Birdie* production, but sleepless nights impaired my ability to sing. Cress's chatterbox proclivities, and her rudeness, were sabotaging my career.

Let me now say three kind things about Cress. Cress knows Russian literature intimately. Cress's botanical renderings—in pencil—win prizes. Cress drinks cabernet franc as opposed to more ubiquitous varietals.

"Nip it in," said Cress, on the phone, at three in the morning. I hugged my pillow; I tried to ignore Cress's conversation, but her phrases, audible through the wall, battered me. "I was hoping to transfer to Crimea, but my boyfriend wanted to move outside." Outside where? Outside Crimea?

Don't think that my life is limited to phobic wars with noisy neighbors. I, too, am an embezzler; I, too, command a position in the world.

The first time I embezzled, I lived in a sugar factory. The second time I embezzled, I worked at a smoke shop on the corner of Caruso Street and Family Lane. The third time I embezzled, I was understudying for the lead in a local *Brigadoon*.

If I'm a pincushion, then Cress is a thimble. Reader, please understand that two personages (Cress and I) star in this story, and that two concrete objects—a pincushion and a thimble— form the nucleus of the story's superego. To placate the superego, we must figure out the relation between the tale's four corners.

Cress sewed me a pantsuit, but I refused to wear it. I hurt Cress's feelings; my capacity to hurt a neighbor's feelings—a neighbor whose all-night conversational extravaganzas, over-heard, destroy my equilibrium—places me on the hit list of any god I'd dare believe in.

Which god do we fear today? The god of telephones? The god of thimbles? The god of morphine? The god of smoke shops? In any smoke shop worth its name, you could see pinned—upon the empyrean billboard—the divine hit list in which I play the starring role, just because I wouldn't wear the pantsuit that Cress kindly sewed for me. The pantsuit obeyed no fashion law I could respect. The pantsuit was not Maoist. The pantsuit was not reminiscent of Yves Saint Laurent. Although every god wanted me to wear the pantsuit, I was born to eschew the clothes that citizens like Cress self-flagellatingly sew for me. Is it my fault that Cress is a self-flagellator?

Zucchini Blossoms

"Don't answer," she said.

I obeyed. Silent, I faced the spectacle of the zucchini blossoms.

"That's why you're an exceptional person," she added. "You have many other good points I hesitate to mention."

I want actual compliments, not feints. I have no liking for Larry, or Todd, or Emery.

All three—Larry, Todd, Emery—huddled around the zucchini blossoms; these plump men were waiting for feedback.

This movie isn't about you, or me, or Larry, or Todd, or Emery.

This documentary focuses on Esther, who remains unaware of her own prominence.

"Don't answer," repeated Esther, uncertain of my compliance.

Many precious substances refuse division. Gold is undivided. Coal is undivided. But Esther is divided.

She is divided between her wish to enforce silence among her paid companions, and her wish to encourage garrulousness.

Whether Esther's self-impersonation instigates a chorus of critical acclaim remains to be seen.

When I have finished considering all the elements awaiting my attention, I will reply to the zucchini blossoms, whose ultimatums—an unspecifiable shade between yellow and orange—terrify any spectator who hasn't forfeited the indwelling moral compass that is native to every human being.

Esther holds the compass in her fist—a fist uncertain of its obligations to the new world order, a regime that extends no courtesies to martyr-goddesses like Esther, who stares into every crystal ball she can find on the clamorous boulevard outside her shelter.

When I grasp Esther's fist, and unclench the fingers, and touch the compass, the oft-mourned "moral compass," the film will end, and the credits—names superimposed over purple stripes, which interfere with legibility—will begin to roll.

Gay Memphis Bookcase

Bob had never been to Memphis, so he felt a certain trepidation when he received, as a gift from his mother, a Gay Memphis Bookcase. Bob wasn't bright, but he was horny. Bob shouted rather than spoke. Bob was on bad terms with his mother, whose generosity continued to pour forth, regardless of Bob's refusal to reciprocate. I could remember, when I first met Bob, the power that simple objects (such as furniture, cloud formations, atlases, mustaches) held over his imagination. I could almost touch his imagination, it was so palpably an element of our conversation, which consisted largely of references to Arlene, his mother. Her outpouring of gifts dominated my first conversation with Bob, who would receive, two years later, this auspicious, terrifying gift of a Gay Memphis Bookcase.

I stood with Bob in his parlor; we beheld the Gay Memphis Bookcase. Was it an ordinary receptacle for books? Was it especially suitable for gay books? Was Bob capable of telling me the defining traits of a gay book? What if the Gay Memphis Bookcase belonged in a chemistry lab? What if the Gay Memphis Bookcase were destined to hold vials of fuming, liquid metals?

Bob took off his jeans and his underwear. He lay on the floor, his buttocks facing me. I didn't have the temerity to ask him why he was gyrating his buttocks. I didn't need to ask. I knew why: the chemicals that his mother had entrusted him with, the chemicals that should now take their rightful place on the Gay Memphis Bookcase, had spilled, in the Ford sedan, when Bob drove me to a cliff's edge to see the sun set over the ocean. Bob had taken too sharp a turn, and the chemical vials, perched lidlessly on the car's back seat, toppled over, spilling their toxic contents on the upholstery. Therefore, no longer did Bob possess chemical vials to place on the Gay Memphis Bookcase that Arlene had thoughtfully sent him.

It was my responsibility to find a new use for the Gay Memphis Bookcase. To please Arlene, I would rescue this piece of furniture from Bob's immature custody.

If I could find a way to get pregnant, I could give birth; if I could give birth, I could buy my infant a chemistry set appropriate for toddlers. My infant could become a toddler mature enough to make use of the chemistry set. I could place the chemistry set, when my toddler wasn't using it, on the Gay Memphis Bookcase. My toddler and I could form an army— an army of two. We could protect the Gay Memphis Bookcase against the classmates that my toddler would eventually meet, the classmates who would make fun of the Gay Memphis Bookcase. To my toddler, I could tell stories about poor limited Bob, who didn't understand his mother's foresight. I could tell stories about Arlene. I could take my toddler on a voyage to Memphis. In Memphis, we could stay in a motel, and I could feed my toddler a bowl of alphabet soup, procured from the motel's restaurant but consumed in our room. Like an orange lozenge and a blue lozenge—throat lozenges, to cure hoarseness—my toddler and I would hover in the sky above the Gay Memphis Bookcase; we would watch over the shenanigans, cheerful but pathetic, that take place whenever a chemistry set overrides its proprietor, whenever a gift cancels its recipient, whenever blue forgets its debt to orange.

Reverse Butterfly

Philadelphia has a largeness that I admire, though I've never been to Philadelphia to test my hypothesis about its size.

I prefer keeping my distance from vast cities, because their beauty has the power to revive my fear of lockjaw.

If I were to travel today to Philadelphia, I would experience a reversal. Let me explain the ethics of reversal.

I have taken a stand, in the past, on the ethical necessity of remaining rigid and never altering one's convictions, even if they are proved wrong. Therefore, within my former system of ethics, to travel today to Philadelphia would involve "reversing my hemispheres," as the Amherst poet might have put it. And my hemispheres, lethargic, don't want to reverse.

So today I stay put in Baltimore and avoid the difficult trip north. I amuse myself, meanwhile, by visiting the butterfly collection in the under-appreciated International Gallery of Butterflies, on North Charles Street, in the basement of a building you might have passed many times without realizing that it contained a neglected treasure, a butterfly collection unrivaled in the state of Maryland.

The proprietor of the International Gallery of Butterflies—I'm ashamed to call him the curator, when he is, as well, the guard and janitor and ticket-booth operator and principal fundraiser—wears Diane von Furstenburg "wrap" dresses to work. His choice of costume receives no commentary in the press. I aim to reverse that silence—to turn neglect into chatter—by publishing this essay in *The Amityville Herald*, if the editors will pamper me.

Years ago I met Diane von Furstenberg at a party, when she came to Baltimore for the premiere of an unfinished film by Max Ophuls, *Watch Me Strut*, which takes place in Baltimore as well as in Anchorage. The flight-to-Eden scenes were filmed in Anchorage. The towering-inferno scenes were filmed in Baltimore. I don't appear in this movie. When I met Diane von Furstenberg, she congratulated me on my butterfly pin, fastened to my lapel. Her cheekbones were so large and so beautiful that I gave her my butterfly pin, or tried to, as a gift of appreciation. She turned away from me at the moment I was considering offering her the pin; in truth, she turned away from me the moment *before* I considered offering her the pin.

The Greenhouse

In the greenhouse, a pink flower lost three of its petals. The pink flower, without a voice, couldn't say farewell to its petals. The pink flower regarded their death with a stony countenance. Does a flower have a face? Does a flower feel sadness? Does a flower understand its lack of words? Does a greenhouse understand the flowers it lodges? If a greenhouse is indifferent to its flowers, could I set up an empathy school, and teach the greenhouse to feel sorrow? Could the pink flower enroll in my empathy school?

These questions, and a few thousand others, occupied my consciousness as I walked toward a greenhouse undergoing its final renovation. Tom, the foreman of the piecemeal operation, had no nationality; nor did any of his construction team. The greenhouse renovation crew had no love for nation-states; the crew, like the pink flower within the greenhouse, feared the arrival of totalitarianism on the palace's grounds. The palace, no longer part of a benign monarchy, had succumbed to a new dictatorial comedian, who'd stolen the palace from the deposed king, and who was initiating a set of reforms that surpassed in cruelty any of the punishments that the king had ever meted out.

I turned my back on the greenhouse; I no longer walked toward its ambiguous, transparent facade. But as I ambled in the opposite direction, I began to mourn the greenhouse's centrality. Even as I continued to abandon the greenhouse, I became, as it were, the greenhouse's dentist; I studied the greenhouse's afterglow—the nimbus formed by the eclipse of the greenhouse from my consciousness—with the myopic fastidiousness of a dentist probing a patient's gums with a pointy implement to see if they will bleed. The greenhouse's metaphorical gums didn't bleed, but I continued to probe them, as I walked, with increasing ferocity and speed, away from the floral sanctuary.

Down the hill, a mile away, I saw the Taffy Hotel, formerly the king's property, and now a prize possession of the dictatorial comedian. I booked a room; I'd stay one night, while I mulled over the greenhouse's complexities.

The next morning, on the hotel's rooftop café, I watched seagulls soar above palace grounds, which weren't near the ocean; seagulls ignored their marine instincts by haunting the once-royal environs, far inland. Hadn't anyone informed the seagulls that a dictatorial comedian had usurped the king's palace, and that therefore the seagulls had no good reason to avoid the sea and concentrate their flight pattern over the manse, its nearby hotel, and the acres of verdant, subtly tamed wilderness that encompassed the kingly demesne?

I canceled plans for the empathy school. Neither the pink flower nor the illogical seagulls would have the opportunity to study under my aegis. I would live, functionless, inside the greenhouse; I would befriend the pink flower, even if it were incapable of reciprocating. I would treat the flower not as my student but as my compatriot, my confessor, my lover, my sales clerk.

Dreams of my omnipotence, like tomatoes, grew on vines impinging on the greenhouse's transparent walls. No one could see the vines, or the dreams growing on them. Of these tomatoes I would make confit; adjectives would season the confit, adjectives more salubrious than allspice or celery salt.

5. *[play our way into utopia]*

Dimples in His Tie

Because his name is Tania, he always has dimples in his tie. His mother and father, who named him after Patty Hearst's revolutionary alias, wanted their son to be a linchpin in the Symbionese Liberation Army, but Tania became a conventional lawyer. That is where we find him today, pursuing his conservative, deposition-taking career, despite the dimples in his tie, which mark him as subversive.

Tania's core muscles, however, are secure. He honed them on the beach, in the exercise booths—bloody cabanas—that line the shore. Tomorrow, he will celebrate the turbulent ocean by hiding inside the cabana and strengthening his abdomen. Tautological yet hale, he considers muscles to be thresholds, dividing the sugary aspects of existence from the cancerous.

Tania wanted to confide in me, but he lacked a confidential streak. He couldn't whisper; he could only bellow. He bellows to rich people, and I'm not rich. So a gulf opened between us, a gulf in which confidentiality could never bloom. The flowers of confidentiality—asters, carnations, mullein— ripped me off by not materializing; they remained spectral. Did I singlehandedly have the power to turn specters into realities? Was I enough of a loudmouth to force an intangible flower to develop an actual stamen and pistil? If I had the ability to blackmail phantom flowers and thereby cajole them into corporealizing, I could wrest confidences from tight-lipped yet bellowing Tania. As if Tania were a catch! I'm not attracted to Tania. I liked his beard, the first time I saw him, but his arrogance turned me off: he wore too much deodorant, and when it dried, it formed unattractive flakes under his arms, like chipped sienna tiles splayed on a mansard roof bombarded by excreting birds.

If I, like Tania, stretch my capacities, who will punish me, as God punished Tania by dimpling his tie? God punished Cain and Eve; God punished the Pharisees and the Sodomites. And after God punishes me, I will write up an account of the faux pas our Creator committed during the scarifying ritual. God thinks that He is in perfect control of his retaliatory routine, but miscalculations mar his stunt; I will itemize those errors in my account, which will become the definitive religious document of our time.

Martha Never Asked Permission Before Dropping By

Martha never asked permission before dropping by. I can't tell you the details with a straight face.

The metropolitan radio station plays oldies, but the city is no longer a viable political identity. Tall ease of towns, we miss you; we miss the thickness of urban self-belief, when avenues trusted their hunches, when plazas countenanced the sunlight in which the unverified guesses gamboled.

And then a phone rang. Its obscene tinkle offended the Blossom Dearie lookalike, my friend, who kept saying "baby" when I mentioned, on Mercer Street, the influence of Godard's *Pierrot le fou* on my liberationist ethos. Revolution must coexist with farce; we must *play* our way into utopia.

The first step toward utopia is to destroy our inheritance's pewter shine.

Martha's maroon parka had motherly seams, like the fissures of her Wedgwood, if Father were to stare at Wedgwood with maternal forbearance. But Father will never stare at Wedgwood with maternal forbearance. That is the tragedy of fathers. Town fathers, bakery fathers, oncology fathers, troubadour fathers, curd fathers—all central fathers dove toward the margin. While diving, they cried out, "My centrality built a fortress in my soul's knee, which cracked open."

Out of the split knee streamed a troupe of Don Bachardy models. Have you seen Bachardy's drawings? The models are often famous, and they are always nude.

Martha bathed her china in a traditional silver nitrate solution; she viewed the china with disdain and wished to solve it, to *chimericalize* it. There is no such word as *chimericalize*, but we have a middling love for this bastard verb, which means *to make a chimera of a solid substance*.

"Uncle, slay me," said Martha, forgetting the encyclopedic riches of her earlier infatuation with Goethe's *Italian Journey*, which I've never read, though I bought it from a man who hugged me after hearing me cry out "I want more and more of you" at a gas station that also sold German literature in translation.

Thrown Crystal

I brushed my teeth in a hurry. I'm thinking about politics all the time, even when I bleed, even when I study Italian grammar. Grammar is the same in all Romance languages. Hence I'm an ideal protester, despite the fact that the toothpaste turned into chewing gum and formed a plaster that stuck to my face. To remove the plaster, I peeled off a layer of my skin. Beneath, I saw a network of rivulets, as if a glass of Waterford crystal, thrown to the floor, had subdivided into patterned waves.

I could ride those waves. Would they welcome me, even if they were merely face-sized? A somewhat male person like me can't ride on his own face, even if it is now composed of oceanic waves.

Ten forests intruded. Remember, in *Macbeth*, the trees of Birnam Wood rising up to overthrow their oppressor? Ten of these Birnam Wood battalions advanced. As they marched, the forests cracked jokes but remained sufficiently arboreal. Dare I repeat their wisecracks? Was I a forest, too, and therefore not in the subordinate position of a mere repeater of witticisms told first and more powerfully by oaks, elms, and cherries?

When the forestry department's dumbfounded chairman (who was, paradoxically, hired to raze forests) strides past my linden-like body, I breathe deeply inward, through my nose, so I can smell his cologne. Something stolid in the way he strides away from me—like a Murphy bed in the process of folding into its wall—assures me that his cologne is Howards End, a fragrance named after a novel I read when I was a smoker, when I tried to delete my lungs rather than protect them.

I tried to delete my eyes and my mouth—by brushing my teeth with a toothpaste that turned into epoxy and adhered to my skin, and by rubbing my dry eyes with a thorn cloth that delicately crazed the corneas. When the Boston Tea Party made its statement, angering the mother country, the waves laughed, and I am now the freckled reincarnation of those happy, revolutionary waves, in a harbor built from contradictory patterns, injudicious cross-hatchings, like a lewd bracelet of sighs worn by a glutton waiting for a ramshackle bus that may never arrive.

Terrifying Typo

I entered the country illegally but was allowed to stay because of a typo on my birth certificate. I can't tell you anything more about the typo, because I don't want to spread the news of my illegitimacy. My unwillingness to talk about the typo leaves us plenty of room for other conversational topics, including recipes for Swedish meatballs. Five meatballs is enough for one person, but I tend to eat at least eight. When I gorge, I feel like a soldier pictured in Géricault's *Raft of the Medusa*. Don't get me started on cannibalism.

The birth certificate with a typo was not genuine, but our Constitution has no provision for distinguishing between real and false documents. The yellow windows of the warehouse building where I now reside are not really yellow; they are gamboge.

If you declare me comatose, I'll lack the power to rebut. Instead of traditional rebuttal, I'll resort to acts of camouflage and mimicry, like a liqueur—Strega—that I've never tasted but that I heard about repeatedly during a riot. I belonged to a rioting cell, a cluster of like-minded dissidents; in this cell, which traveled around the city, from riot to riot, liqueurs were often mentioned but never consumed. Mentioning liqueurs was a decoy procedure, but we also had deep affinity with the liqueurs we cited. My friend Figo never faked his love for Strega, when he whispered "Strega" to me in the heat of riot. How do I know that his murmuring lullaby of "Strega"—as if to put me to sleep in the middle of combat—was intended specifically for me, and was not an anthem sung to all incendiaries congregated on Battery Street? Would the other revolutionaries feel as strongly about the word *Strega* as I did? Would the word be wasted on them?

Impure was my heart, and yours, too, was impure, shot through with impertinence. What is impertinence? Nothing you can taste. Nothing you can buy. Impertinence arises, like flame from a match, when the flame decides it loves the match and therefore wishes to materialize, hotly, to demonstrate this love. The love of a flame for its inciting match is not frequently celebrated by those officials in charge of deciding which loves will be blazoned and which will be silenced.

The Logic of Rivulets

She drove a dented Pontiac to deliver my paintings. I wasn't the painter; I was merely the purchaser. The paintings were floral studies of alumni. She—the dealer—drove a Pontiac to deliver paintings I'd bought on hearsay. I'm comfortable buying art I've never seen, but I'm not comfortable with flawed vehicles.

The first round of battle with the dealer went well. With a squeaky voice, like Minerva Mouse's, she apologized for the Pontiac. I belligerently directed the conversation, and she scowled at my pugilism. I've been reading up on gerbils; by imbibing rodent consciousness, I'll become an expert in effortful aesthetics.

I wreaked havoc in December, though the small man riding in the back of the Pontiac ignored me; he snubbed me in December, and he kept on snubbing me in January, when the floral studies were delivered. Why do small men ignore me in Havana? When and why are you leaving Havana? Because you want the hotel experience to end? Or do you want to amortize your own thighs? Amortize them, so that they might approach the rivulets you tried to describe yesterday—the canceled rivulets, like beds that sleep four. In the mattress of each canceled rivulet could sleep four children, if you gave them morphine. I'm not the right bookie to dispense the morphine; my morality is too fixed.

Breakfast in the hotel was ham and cheese. The concierge gave me advice on which cathedrals to visit, which Beckett plays to perform, which skin tags to remove. When you enter Valhalla you need to tear your ticket, to prove that you are causal, that your birth leads to your death. Because I'm a communist, I depise normative currency, including Bloomingdale's house-brand cutlery. I converted to communism in Berlin, when happenstance led me to the meadow where Rosa Luxemburg was murdered. For Rosa I converted. And for Rosa I keep speaking. For Rosa I pursue the logic of rivulets, even if I can't master that logic, even if I can't define *rivulet*.

He Is Perpetually Tan

A failure of empathy, like a saxophone refusing to differentiate between post-soul and pre-soul, afflicted the psychiatrist on winter afternoons.

I am not the psychiatrist, but I am the sax, in human form, distantly vibrating, my shirt untucked. Parts of my body are not well-socialized; these vibrating regions lack empathy.

Their stoniness—a piece of errant, hurtful legislation—passes through Congress's gullet.

So I took a job. Whoever utters such a sentence is a bicyclist unloading his erotic coffers in tiny, aggressive, "night-versus-day" spurts—gaseous emissions, like a mourning scree.

What does "night-versus-day" mean to the smiling barrister? Is he smiling because he has been fired?

"Night-versus-day" means that if you are gay, you go out at night and are perpetually tan. False certainties demonstrate my lack of empathy. A sign now points me toward the mountain.

Toward the mountain I cheerfully amble. The mountain-oriented dwarves, who lure borderlines like me toward the peaks, said that the alpine restaurants will serve butter cakes only in the afternoons, and that if I don't time my visit carefully, I will miss the butter-cake interludes. The dwarves—

logicians manqués—know that butter equals salvation. I am in the process of giving up my religious beliefs.

It began to rain as I crawled up the steep road. If Ava Gardner's granddaughter lived in the mountain-top lodge, I wouldn't be surprised, but what could I do with that information, except weep? Weeping is the symptom that consigned me to this queasy vocation of climbing, ambling, arguing, stripping, keening. Why is everyone on this mountain trail—everyone except for me—conspicuously pious? Are we on the verge of the Vatican?

This notecard, on which I'm inkily litanizing, contains micro-traces of hemp. I can't assume that my facade of psychosis will alter the cruel political landscape.

I linger on this lip—this borderline—of psychosis because a rooster can't crow without my cooperation. What rooster? *That* rooster, the one over there, the stolid bird taking a correspondence-school class in how to crow. And therefore I love the rooster and can claim to empathize with a creature cramming for its exam.

The spell lifts; Martha Stewart, or Stan Getz, or Stan Laurel's grandfather, is the momentary cantor, making melisma of my ascension to the ranks of souls who experience empathy.

I, too, have cantorial tendencies. Notice how a nugget of self-disgust arises like a wall, or like Tom Snout impersonating a wall in *A Midsummer Night's Dream*.

Stan Laurel's heir gave me his recently published chapbook about Miami, an incendiary poem, French phrases mingling with Ladino. Have you noticed that Laurel's heir waddles? His heft retroactively complicates the starry progenitor's thin fame.

Let me conclude by praising Stan Laurel. He worked harder than most comedians whose careers left verifiable traces, sycamores in a sacred moonlit grove supervised by Sappho. Sappho doesn't spoil the conclusion. "Jason," she said, "if you were alone in this grove, if you were unsupervised, you would not be capable of writing a poem. You would not have political wisdom to offer the people of Miami. You would not be balm at this historic moment when the liberties of Miami and all similar metropolises are being threatened by the newly arriving bloated prince, the prince who never recognizes me or says hello, though he always arrives in the grove promptly at 11:30 in the morning and erases a few million people's identities by spraying a cloud of toxic foam over their birth certificates and medical records." Sappho, in small doses, cured me. Empathy permits me to write this feeble sentence.

Is Stan Laurel to blame? Are you a cantor? Is Sappho alive? Am I perpetually tan? More restful and endless questions have never been murmured within earshot of fallen nobility. And if I am that nearly decapitated queen, then you are the danger-seeking guttersnipe who leads us up the mountain toward the butter-cake lodge, where rumor reigns.

Why do men with red hair keep walking by the window? Are they, too, involved in the butter-cake conspiracy?

I knew Guy #1, but I didn't recognize Guy #2. Both had stubble. Their mystique, like a charley horse, crackled on the soundtrack. Non-recognition, too, crackled, at the moment when the soundtrack stopped synchronizing with the lip movements of the principal actors. When synchronization ends, ecstasy begins.

6. *[a revolutionary almanac torn to pieces]*

The Temple of Timidity

I lay on my back in the darkness. The prosecutor would arrive when I'd waited long enough, with sufficient timidity. But how could timidity be measured, and what functionary could be trusted to do the measuring? No almanac or atlas graced my night table; no dictionary could lead me to the etymology (and thereby into the logic) of *timidity*, its sepulchral din, its chemical composition, and its movie theaters.

Within the temple—unseen—of my timidity, that suddenly overpopulated abstraction, I bought a ticket at the movie theater and started watching a western. Its star was some modern equivalent of Cliff Robertson, who specialized in playing delicate, psychotic men. The character's delicacy was always at odds with his psychosis; you could forgive the malevolence because his quivering skinny arms, his eyes pooling with tears, convinced you that he had been a victim of child abuse, if only at the overworked hands of bus drivers and French tutors.

The Western I was watching, in the movie theater nestled within the temple of timidity, ended, and I decided not to stay for the second half of the double feature. A woman I'd met on the way to the theater had said, "If I fix your melancholy, will you give me a hug?" She'd made this simple offer with such aplomb, such nonchalance, and such a leer, as if she were a figure in a Kirchner painting, that I'd taken her business card, and lightly promised that I'd meet her in the kitchen of the restaurant she managed, a sandwich shop on the Plaza Beauregard. I found the manager, as promised, in the kitchen; removing the sanitary gloves she'd donned to help her minions prepare sandwiches, she guided me down the back stairs into a small unlit office. She was wearing light blue pants, which made me skeptical of her intentions; how could a restaurant manager in pale blue be trusted to fix my melancholy or sate my hunger for illicit caresses in dreamy surroundings?

In her basement office, I lay down on the floor, as she'd commanded. She took off her questionable pants, and I allowed her to remove my skirt, stockings, underwear, bra, shirt, backpack, earrings, watch, and eyeglasses. I lay there, within the overseeing vicinity of a black mirror, whose relation to my body could never be decided or described. Were I to decode the mirror's power over my nudity, I'd be forced to climb the stairs, cross the kitchen, exit the restaurant, hurry through the overcrowded Plaza Beauregard, find again the obscure movie theater that seemed to be open for customers only in the evenings, buy a ticket, sit through a western flick whose star seemed a copy of Cliff Robertson, somnambulate out of the theater, and seek the hidden passageway back into the foyer of the temple of timidity, where I could request admission to the original room in which you had forced me to lie down and wait for the prosecutor, whose mission, and whose arrival time, were recorded in a revolutionary almanac I'd long ago torn to pieces.

Profile of a Departed Cellist

Darling, I'm trying to reproduce, in words, the time we pressed our groins together on the beach. You were attempting to console me; I'd been fired from *Vogue*.

Later, when we returned to the city, I went back to *Vogue*'s office and discovered that I'd been granted a stay of execution. But, do you remember, you came with me, to *Vogue*, and stood near me in the hallway outside the editor's office; and when she offered me a chance to write a profile on Jacqueline du Pré, and I tried to explain that the unparalleled cellist had died long ago, you quickly intervened?

You and I leaned against the vitrine of trophies that *Vogue* had won in the journalism wars; once more, as on the beach, we pressed our groins together. This frottage—this out-of-place friction—partook of the journalism war's amorality; we, like fourth-estate warriors, had lost touch with Hannah Arendt's belief that anti-Semitism catalyzed totalitarianism. We were not bigots; we were not readers of political theory. We were gossips, flirts, hacks—unemployed tricksters, trying to cop a feel in the corridors of power. Would we succeed in hijacking power, or would sovereignty kick us in the gallbladder?

Now came the moment when you brought out your camera. Many times before, you'd photographed me—nude, clothed, unweeping, driving, carousing, on divans, on trampolines, in cabooses, near verandas. You'd photographed me in every variation suggested by Josef Albers in his guide to posing—his vanished treatise on how bodies, when placed athwart each other, leak chiaroscuro, like a trickle of motor oil beginning to form a milky skin in the Texas light.

Here, in the *Vogue* hallway, you took my picture. I tell people only a certain amount of our sexual history. By omitting details, I become a *mistress of parts*, a segmenter, whose actions of cropping have a somberness to be found in the Book of Daniel, if Nina Simone were to sing it.

Outside the editor's office, I leaned against a mirror. My right nipple, reflected in the opaque glass, rebuked every totalitarian tenet of the media's war against my sovereign desire. My desire retained sovereignty by pretending to ignore your camera. I revealed too much of myself by feigning indifference to your Leica. Health, as Arendt knew, came from a mirror-like integration between soul and body; because my soul was tainted not only by frottage in a *Vogue* hallway but by my aggressive distortions, my weal would disintegrate.

I'm trying to reproduce this disintegration for you, today, because at heart I am a character in a collage by Jess, and I can't exit the collage, except by fervent, exacting speech. If you would put down your camera, look me in the eye, break your fast, and say "I recognize you," I could continue my subtle acts of warfare against stillness and ossification.

Later that afternoon, we returned to the beach, one hundred miles outside the city. I drank a milkshake, purchased on the boardwalk; and you found, in the milkshake (or so you would tell me, in the future) an echo of the solicitude I'd long ago shown you, in an early bedroom scene, when I'd kissed your flanks. How the residue of lost solicitude—a memory of flank-kissing—can surface again in a milkshake sipped on a winter beach is a puzzle that only Jacqueline du Pré's unreleased recording of *Kol Nidre* can solve.

Do You Take Mustard?

She observed me while I slept.

"Do you take mustard?" she asked.

"Take mustard where, take mustard how?" I replied, in my sleep, but half-awake already, eager to begin the day.

Would my eagerness please her, or would it cause her to ruin the photographs while developing them? And would my fans, seeing the ruined photographs, think that I'd lost my grip on beauty, a regime that had been dear to me in the first years of the new century?

Now I shall reminisce about our early years together, when toilets were a problem. We were living in a substandard apartment, with faulty plumbing. We had a plumber friend, inert in temperament, and like a forsythia in her tendency to express joy in strangely timed outbursts. Think of the season's last forsythia—its hectic refusal to accept a realistic prognosis of imminent death. That was our plumber, in essence; you can imagine how our toilet suffered.

That forsythia—that plumber, that toilet—entered my sleep this morning, as my companion addressed to me her enigmatic question about mustard: whether I took mustard, whether I refused it, whether I needed to bone up on mustard, conquer its intricacies and saliences.

Nancy Reagan, at that point in history—the era of the forsythia—was still alive, though only once or twice a year would her photo, in the newspaper, provoke in me a spasm of retributive rage, as if Mrs. Reagan, even merely in a photograph, constituted an outer borough of my consciousness. Could I continue to function as a spokesperson for ecological equilibrium, for filling buckets and then emptying them, for frequenting nightclubs and then coming home to read textbooks about positivism all night long?

Later, you and I lived in Paris; around us, remedies for stomach ailments seemed to proliferate, appearing in shop windows, in magazine ads, and in the conversations we overheard while walking through the Park des Buttes-Chaumont, where, at the Temple of the Sibyl, we reconsecrated our vows to keeping the utmost secrecy, together, about our customs and tastes, the strange (some would say infernal) rituals that occupied our nights, the necromancies (intrinsically virginal) that intensified our muscular powers, and our abilities to contract, retract, and protract.

Nothing ever happened *to* us; all events stemmed from our own ferocious actions—contortions of arm and leg, fluencies of riposte, cruelties of delayed execution. The small actions that constituted our necromantic toolkit—our daily roster of performances, however unseen—proceeded with the same directionless passivity that had predetermined our flight to Paris, and that then had occasioned our expulsion from Paris, and our shamed return to the apartment in the sunny valley of an imperiled Western state, a state endangered, in part, by our own mercilessly attenuated aggressions, candle-lit flickerings that glanced off the reflective surfaces of this cell, perpetually shrouded in a darkness that you have engineered, a darkness to which you will sacrifice my prone, dream-stunned body.

Decor Analysis

The drapes interfered with Martha's view of the ceiling's tranquilizing blankness. She resented the drapes, though she had chosen them. The history of Martha's distaste for drapes had no politics, though she'd often attempted to gild the lily of her drape resentment by imposing a political narrative on it.

The mirror, in her bedroom, reflected half of a soulful window. The window's capacity to withstand tempest had limits; Martha knew these limits because she had created them. She habitually curtailed the liberties of the objects surrounding her. "To curtail," she often said, "is to love."

While lying in bed, Martha listened to a radio station playing dismal oldies. An appetite for the dismal had always characterized Martha's leisure hours, if an observer were to stand above her leisure hours—to look down on them from an angelic perch—and comment upon their moral complexion.

Martha was not alone in the bedroom. A woman had come to join Martha tonight; the visitor stood in the shadow of a doorway, and had, as of yet, no voice. She was waiting for Martha to lend her a voice, but Martha was not in the lending mood.

I am not usually in the position of pontificating about Martha's desires; I prefer to reserve my pontifical energies for decor analysis.

Martha is more than decor. The voiceless visitor to Martha's bedroom is more than decor. I, however, am less than decor—less worthy, less symbolic, less freighted with consciousness—and so I bridge the distance between decor and me by analyzing. The more I analyze decor, the closer I come to its threshold.

Martha's room is composed of triangles. I, as a decor analyst, necessarily play the role of hypotenuse. No lust obtains between the hypotenuse and Martha. The hypotenuse may try to drum up an erotic charge, but the hypotenuse will fail.

The triangles in Martha's room resemble Napoleon Bonaparte, Mao Zedong, and Eva Hesse. All three had triangular aspects. To explain these features would lead me back to Martha's chosen radio station, the one playing dismal oldies; I would become a dismal oldie, though at least I would have the privilege of insinuating a path into Martha's ears. Relinquishing my position as decor analyst, I would become a Pied Piper of Martha-consciousness; I would become a syrinx, a harmonica, a thumb piano, or one of those strange devices formerly known as a Jew's harp, a term that long ago passed into disrepute—the Valley of Disrepute, in which I continue, pliantly, to dwell.

An Exercise in Expiation

If I returned to her room, would I find her on the bed, or would she be hiding under it? Would I be responsible for her position?

Five years ago, when I made tomato soup for her, she berated me because I hadn't added turkey.

My avoidance of turkey began long ago, but I lack the leisure at this moment to discuss my appetites and aversions.

If I returned to her bedroom, could I dictate her actions, or would she script mine?

*

I am addressing this message to you because, in the past, you sympathized when I complained about my lover, who has now invited me to return to her bedroom for an exercise in expiation.

*

I have never been your lover. You made a pass at me at the book fair. I was afraid of the book fair; you took my fear, and made a medley of it. Into that medley you inserted a hand. A medley is not a physical object; it is an abstraction. Nonetheless, my fear, at the book fair, assembled itself into a medley, as if by Henry Mancini, who composed the score for *Touch of Evil*, your favorite movie. The medley-in-me—call it the MM, or the MiM—seemed to contain an opening, and into that opening you inserted your hand.

I am addressing this message to you because you advised me against returning to the photographer's bedroom—the photographer, my former amour. A flashing light within your refusal—as if your refusal were to divide in half, and a strobe light were to install itself in the seam where your refusal's two moons exchange vows—woke me up to my predicament's seriousness.

Amnesia occupied my predicament's center: amnesia about my love affair with the photographer, and amnesia about the "book," a species with which I no longer have truck.

But the flashing light, aforementioned, has vaguely the power to revive my dread of interstate highways; I fear their beauty, their complexity, their flatness, their rage, their historical situatedness, and their grime. Highways bind me to the labyrinth I inhabit when the photographer telephones, asking me to return to her bedroom.

*

Much later, I recited this monologue with a Calabrian accent. I wore a fake fur coat: a perfect costume for delivering an impermissible diatribe. You declared it impermissible because you enjoyed the theatrics of cutting me off in the middle of a sentence.

Conversation in Darkness

You had a tendency, like Monica Vitti, to lean forward.

Were you afraid I'd topple?

Monica Vitti never toppled. She stayed upright, even while leaning.

But were you afraid that I would lack Vitti's poise, and would end up collapsing?

Your potential collapse was always on my mind, though I rarely gave it utterance.

Did your addiction to fancy talk begin in childhood?

My mother was a fancy talker.

And your father?

Father was a procrastinator.

Talk was the ordeal he feared, and therefore he procrastinated?

Yes, darling, he feared talk.

I miss the days when you called me darling.

Your exactness of pitch excites me, always has.

Pitch is subjective. I don't like to be judged by subjective factors.

Right. You prefer objective scrutiny, even with the cruelty that objective examiners tend to pile upon the scene of scrutiny.

Are you comfortable in the nude?

I take my clothing cues from Rousseau.

Was he a nature-loving sort?

He couldn't face the music of his own proleptic nudism. His nudism posthumously ate away at the nineteenth century, which tried to pretend it was immune to internal varmints.

Now I'm confused, sweetheart. If you like nudism, why do you castigate it as a breeding-ground for varmints and laziness?

Laziness and varmint-consciousness are part of the big picture I'm assembling here in this bedroom.

I take it, then, that varmint-consciousness, your fancy term for "inner turmoil," is always an option, even when we're supposedly studying hard for our exams.

Which exams do you mean, darling?

The one we're taking right now.

I don't think that we're in midst of an exam. We're just lying here nude, trying to recapture some vanished essence.

Nudity is always an exam. The mind is examining the body. One breast is examining the other breast. The lamplight is examining the eyebrow. The buttocks are joined together to grade the exam.

But the pleasure of being with you again, here in this bedroom, is that no one is grading our rapport. No one is standing above it, in a position of omniscience, determining whether it succeeds or fails.

I like to give myself credit for omniscience.

Is there such a thing as a non-sexy omniscience?

No. It's always sexy to know, always sexy to spy, always sexy to partake of someone else's consciousness, especially if that person thinks that her consciousness is ringed round by impenetrable fences.

I don't consider myself the fenced-in type. Most of our life together, we've dispensed with walls.

Dislike of walls was your contribution.

Yes, I was the queen of wall removal.

You insisted on a transparency that often worked as an anti-aphrodisiac.

You weren't turned on by my see-through consciousness.

Sometimes I needed a pebble, as it were, to stand in the way of perfect viewing.

I did not stint on pebbles.

But you insisted that I ask for the pebble. You never offered a pebble of your own accord.

A gratis pebble is not perfectly a pebble.

You wanted me to pay for my pebble by begging for it.

Yes, I wanted a plea from your mouth, in your own words, to substantiate the pebble and to make it froth.

A pebble can't froth.

Disagree. The obstructions to perfect visibility are often in a frothing state.

The fences froth?

Yes. The walls, separating my mind from yours, are capable of perptual foam.

And so the foam abets the obstruction? The foam decreases transparency?

Yes, the foam impinges on our omniscience.

Did the foam make you feel more nude, or less nude?

Nudity bookends my consciousness, whether or not I'm capable of soaring to Olympian heights.

So nudity is the alpha and omega of your inwardness?

Yes. Without nudity, I'd have no alphabet.

Can there be consciousness without an alphabet to delineate it?

An alphabet doesn't delineate consciousness. An alphabet creates consciousness.

When's the last time you washed this mirror?

I sprayed it with Fantastik this morning.

You forgot to wipe it off with a paper towel. The cleaning fluid left little pockmarks all over the glass.

Why castigate those harmless flecks by calling them pockmarks?

Because I was raised in the nineteenth century, with echoes of Rousseau.

And so plague is part of your vocabulary.

Plague is my mooring.

You couldn't think without plague to help you out.

Without plague as a category, I couldn't function. Not even in a cocktail lounge.

To flirt, you need plague?

I need plague in order to know that I am I, and you are you.

I lack plague. Maybe that's why I'm so confused about you and me.

Plague takes sophistication. You need to be born with it.

The pockmarks on the mirror are part of plague?

Plague is where sight begins, and where it falters.

I'm not sure that this conversation has prevented me from faltering.

When you stop faltering, I will cease to love you.

Is my porousness an essential part of what you love?

What I love most about you is your near-invisibility.

And were I fully to materialize, you'd grow disenchanted?

———————

The excitement built. And then it subsided. Later, ardor would again ascend, but no one would be present to report on it.

7. *[the civic crotch]*

Pillow and Tom

Into the land of grapes we went with a pillow and with Tom; but Tom was a hairy top, or that is how he advertised himself, and grapes would not compensate him for the pillow's forfeitures. Please explain what you mean by forfeitures. Tom would not explain, and the pillow (which resembled a deflated dumpling) could not explain. Because Tom escorted me on all my travels, the pillow occupied the role of "odd man out," though the pillow was not a man and was not odd. The pillow blessedly hewed to convention.

This pillow in particular was silver on the outside and lime on the inside. As Tom's assailant, I had no complaint to make about the pillow. And yet the pillow, unlike a condom, couldn't protect me against Tom's syphilis; nor could the pillow declare a truce in my battle against the hegemony of grapes. Many were the cottages wherein Tom plied his "top" wares, and he had come to the land of grapes (under my hostile wing) to distribute his "top" mentality as widely as possible around a country saddened by its own distance from the euro and from Oz. Tom, as "top," partook of Oz—and so perhaps he would unify the grapes? Would Tom make the many grapes—the too many grapes—one woe?

All of us—in the whore contingent traveling between grapes and Thee—occupied the position of that silver pillow, a pillow I falsely promised you would be the center of this tale. I meant to honor the pillow as a friend but have instead desecrated it—as if it were an urn I'd never kissed, a pillow-urn I'd never allowed to smother me. Every pillow wishes to smother the speaker who leads it into the realm of grapes, and Tom is not less hairy or mercantile because of my failure.

Newspaper on a Dubious Patio

The newspaper in his hand contained sexual advertisements, although the Tampa Municipal Council had outlawed them. The man holding the newspaper in his sweaty palm had recently moved to Tampa for the purpose of joining a law firm famous for its habit of shrinking already small businesses into even more minuscule size. (The law firm belonged to a political movement that wished the corporate landscape to be at once simplified and decimated.) The newspaper's sexual advertisements had no pictures; picturelessness caused the man to cease loving the newspaper he held in his hand. At that precise moment, a woman whose carnival career consisted in doing Ethel Kennedy impersonations entered the law firm's overcrowded canteen, where our protagonist Alessandro Peacock stood, immobilized, as if staring at a solar eclipse.

In response to the Ethel Kennedy look-alike's silent incredulity (she seemed to be drooling), Alessandro said, "You'd often begged me to join your carnival act, but I don't resemble your late husband, so my presence in the ring would confuse the audience. Earlier this morning I hallucinated that the newspaper in my hand had no contents. It had become a blank slab of greasy paper, without words or images. For that blankness, I may be pilloried." The Ethel Kennedy look-alike no longer resembled Ethel Kennedy. The vanishing—or depletion—of the former resemblance caused our momentary protagonist to doubt whether he would long remain in the employ of a law firm whose collection of Dubuffet sculptures—one on the lawn, one in the lobby, one in the roof-deck lounge, and one in the basement gym—deterred readers of this or any dying tale from regretting the ease with which back-page sexual advertisements reflected the groin habits and ocular melancholies binding us to our sun-drenched, prostrate bodies, arrayed on a dubious patio, three miles west of here.

Mayoral Chandelier

The chandelier in the mayor's dining room was insufficiently mayoral, an insufficiency that displeased the mayor's father, who had bestowed upon his only son this gilded chandelier as a symbol of the civic crotch that the son must now nurse to maturity. The chandelier had no say in the matter; the chandelier, more bisexual than most lamp fixtures, cared for neither civics nor degeneration. Degeneration would be the fate of the civic crotch, if the indifferent chandelier did not step up to bat by mitigating its own brilliancy, by deciding to grow dim at accustomed hours, and by desiring the civic crotch and thus preventing the mayor from pox. Pox awaited the mayor, if his father didn't rise from narcoleptic coma and aid the chandelier in limiting its illumination. In this dining room, before coma had incapacitated the mayor's father, the two would often sit, over postprandial cordials, and bash the populace through slur and banter. I was sometimes present at these colloquies, under the watchful light of a chandelier whose function the apothecary and the plumber had grown to doubt. I never doubted the chandelier. I was its staunch defender, its medicator. I applied grease and toothpick to the crevices within the chandelier's unseen foundations, where the chandelier ceased to be entirely a chandelier, and began to resemble a grotto within Paris's honeycombed sewers. Because my affair with the mayor's father had offended the newspaper's editorial staff, I had no choice but to lubricate the chandelier, and to sit on lucky evenings with the mayoral *père et fils* to contemplate the wreckage of the town asleep around us, a town already so afflicted with caries and rot, that soon we would have no cabinet, no police, no mansion, and no chandelier. Meanwhile, the mayor wrote his speeches under the glaucous pools of light the chandelier sent downward in its quest to be an ambassador of civility. Nine limbs had the chandelier; the mayor and I would soon bury the father, burn his papers, and try to forget the red boat he long ago rowed on the village's lake. A lithograph of this boat sold last night at Sotheby's. After the sale, the victorious purchaser celebrated her triumph at a tapas bar where the portions were criminally meager.

The Diplomatic Rock

A rock interposed itself between China and Norway, according to the retired diplomat. No one accepted his judgment, so he rescinded it.

The retired diplomat longed to lie in bed with Marcello in that diamond magnate's Arts and Crafts villa, in Fiesole Heights, on a street surrendering to gentrification.

I am the retired diplomat. The country I represented, during my diplomatic career, had no name. Or else most players on the world stage found my underdog country's name impossible to pronounce.

A rock interposed itself between the swimming pool and the cabanas. Some swimmers, passing by the rock, would rub their hands on the rock's surface; the rock was thought to bring good luck to those who dared to rub it.

I stepped out of retirement. I rejoined the diplomatic corps of my unpronounceable land. I exited cabana number four—the cabana most shadowy, most compromised, most overstocked with terrycloth towels and mildewed slippers—and stopped, en route to the pool, at the bewildering rock, as tall as a child, as wide as a fire hydrant, as gray as a painting by Whistler. I rested my scented palms on the rock's gritty surface. I rubbed my fingers along its visible seams—as if the rock had cracked in transit, on the mail truck that had delivered it to this aquatic compound, where I gravely oscillated between retirement and employment.

Marcello surprised me by suddenly appearing, here, at the rock. Had his villa been destroyed by fire? What else could explain his heretical, tearful visit to a rock I'd thought it my sole duty to fondle?

At this troubled juncture in the narrative, we no longer find ourselves in Fiesole Heights. We are now—and perhaps we have always been—on a rocky island somewhere between Norway and China. Here, where waves crash against cliffs loved by no world leaders, I place my well-traveled and argumentative hands on a gray rock; I hope that its ridges will puncture my cosseted palms and cause them to bleed. Blood will authorize me to push my love for Marcello toward physical rapture and rescue us from the arid zone of diplomatic quibbling. If Marcello remains with me at this "shrine of the rock," with its Ennio Morricone soundtrack, then I will cease oscillating between eclipse and appearance. I will save my unpronounceable country's honor. I will give head to Marcello. I will repair this narrative's deplorable inconsistencies. I will emulate, in stability and emotional nullity, the rock I have been cherishing and avoiding. The rock will be mine, and no portion of my psyche or my physique—an otter's—will be unrocklike.

We were alone with the retired diplomat, in cabana number four, as he recited this circuitous and troubled tale. Our job was to represent the rock's rights and wishes, which stood in opposition to the diplomat's. Nausea, an obbligato, accompanied us as we ministered to the diplomat and protected our rock-client's rights. We performed our paradoxical duties by fantasizing about nude Marcello while injecting embalming fluids into the veins of the diplomat's corpse-cold recitation.

8. *[impersonate the tree]*

Gauffrage and the Erotic Limitations of Capability Klein

A boy on the way to school asked a tree, "What is gauffrage?" The tree answered, "Gauffrage is an embossing technique found in Japanese woodblock prints." Of course the tree was not an elm or an oak. The tree was a docent, trained in Ithaca. The boy was too young to appreciate the niceties of woodblock prints. The boy was interested in dildos, however, because he had looked up *dildo* in the encyclopedia on his teacher's desk, a one-volume encyclopedia, a glum book, without humor or kindness.

The boy would postpone his encounter with dildos and with gauffrage until he was thirty years old, and employed in a mattress store. I am the owner of the mattress store, but I farm out its management to responsible caretakers. My main caretaker, who looks exactly like Rosalind Russell, hired the dildo-haunted boy, now a man, to work as salesman. Our mattress store is located on a busy intersection in downtown Taormina, New York, a town in the Catskills, where the well water is polluted but the fish markets carry untainted offerings.

The salesman, Capability Klein, known as "Cap," works on his dildo collection in the evenings. During the day, he devotes himself to the mattress store, where he holds the record for most mattresses sold per day: three.

Cap and I are bowling buddies: Saturday nights, we bowl in Taormina's less popular alley. There are two bowling alleys in Taormina; Cap and I prefer the alley that attracts fewer customers.

Last night, after bowling, we repaired to his backyard, where we discussed the limitations that interfere with Cap's ability to experience erotic pleasure. Cap did not phrase the issue in that punitive fashion. He did not describe these characteristics as limits. He called them "talking points." With all my heart I wish to be an organized narrator, and so I will list the talking points without editorial commentary. To do so, I must impersonate the tree—or docent—who first served the role of interlocutor, when Cap was a curious boy, walking to school, accompanied by a guardian who often behaved in such a stiff and wooden manner, and with such undulations of leaf and pendencies of bough, that the boy judged the docent to be a vertical adjudicator with the firmness and coldness of an ancient oak.

Last night Cap told me that he wanted to suck on the toes of women and men wearing shoes that raised the wearer several inches off the wormy floor. The shoes, according to Cap, should be elevated, open-toed mules: genderless, transparent, hieratic.

I grow suddenly reluctant to say more about Cap's erotic limits; this reluctance takes a physical form, like the impressed portions of a page surrendering to gauffrage, an action that leaves the influenced areas blank, because no pigment is applied to those regions of the woodblock print. My reluctance to say more about Cap's sexual limits manifests itself as a headache, as if my forehead were the victim or beneficiary of gauffrage.

Last night, in Cap's backyard, we could see, wandering across the grass, three skunks, each accompanied by a carmine cloud. Carmine is not usually fluorescent. These clouds disobeyed the laws of carmine, and acquired an unnatural day-glow brilliance that wounded the eye lucky enough to gaze at their felicities. The clouds emitted by the skunks did not yet stink, but I understood that I was to blame for the imminent foul smell that would taint Cap's backyard for the rest of the evening. The skunks somehow knew of my arrival at Cap's house, and had come to haunt his backyard as a result of my own unacknowledged prurience.

Cap assured me, in a calm voice, that I was not to blame for the skunks. However, when I saw two deer running across his backyard, I knew that Cap was in cahoots with the animal kingdom, and that this relation of "cahoots" was a symptom of his mental decline. I could replenish Cap's capacities by becoming a more trustworthy elucidator of his erotic limits, as I had earlier promised you.

I don't want Cap to die of Lyme disease—a real possibility, if he doesn't overcome his love for animals. What we, in Taormina, call Lyme, is a combination of other afflictions, so our Lyme is not the nation's or the world's Lyme, but a local variety, connected to the animals that frequent our backyards and make Taormina a town often studied by progressive scientists seeking to destroy the complacencies that limit custom-bound epidemiologists.

I am enchanted by the possibilities of nonfiction in Taormina. We are a hub of truth-telling and accuracy. Our mattresses are like Leda, in Yeats's great poem. Our mattresses, the ones sold in my store, are vulnerable foam, though they uphold bodies permitted to be monstrous in size and inclination. Tourists and residents shop for mattresses in my store, and Capability Klein gives them a service they couldn't find in the original Taormina, that tired town in Sicily. The Sicilian Taormina is our namesake; we are the newfangled copy, which improves on the original, as a piece of dull paper is improved by a violent embossing procedure that wreaks havoc on the page's flat suppositions. Cap's most egregious erotic limit is his confusion about where the second vagina is located on women and where the second anus is located on men. The second vagina and the second (male) anus are virtuous waystations in the conversations held by prurient customers of my mattress store, where Cap overhears fine points of anatomy, controversial relocations of genital landmarks; but he must remain speechless about these matters while he is under my jurisdiction.

Let me end this small summary of local events by reminding you that, because I am the narrator (or custodian) of this account, I have a bad odor. The smell surrounding me is thick, like a gelatinous soup made worse by cornstarch. But within my bad odor there exist pockets of refinement and oasis, where you could rest between scenes, while you wait for your return plunge into the mal-olfactory, or Maillol Factory, *Mal Oeil* Factory, or Oiled Male Factory. Mere wordplay! Such antics distract me from disclosing the nature of the dildos that already preoccupied young Capability Klein when he was walking, in a haze of confusion, to school, and asking the docent-tree to define the tricky process known as gauffrage. To those early dildos I will eventually return. Perhaps I have never left their circumference. Perhaps my consciousness is circumscribed by the dildos that Cap Klein never understood, the dildos that Cap never knew how to apply to the practice of everyday life, or to the psychogeography of melting Arctic sea ice. Can you help Cap out with his problem? Can you explain the dildos? Can you explain the melting ice? Can you bring the two regimes of meaning—dildos, ice—together? Or is it time for me to retire from running a mattress store whose ledgers don't balance? Is it time for Cap's parents to rise from the grave and help their son exterminate the skunks and deer that plague his yard and give rise to waking nightmares? Poor phobic Cap, worrying himself to death over three skunks.

Who Speaks?

Ezekiel turned on the cassette recorder; he wanted to destroy the conversation in which he was taking part, and the best way to decimate an encounter was to record it. Today, in April 1978, a lack of conviction forced Ezekiel to blow his nose on a page from the *Christian Science Monitor*, to which his mother had given him a lifetime subscription. The cassette recorder stopped functioning; it shook, made a series of ominous clicks, and then the tape's forward motion halted. Ezekiel's lover, Ugo, a young man who worked for a prestigious publisher, said, "The machine is broken." Issuing this bland statement of fact, Ugo sounded distressed, or so Ezekiel thought; Ezekiel worried too frequently, and with an unattractive obsessiveness, about his lover's inner life. Ugo, despite his enviable job at the nation's leading publisher of vaudevillian missals, had a track record of mental instability that had caused his employers no small amount of anguish during his first months at the firm. "I think it's best if we leave our conversation unrecorded," said Ezekiel, who had recently accepted a job as librarian at the university's medical school, which boasted four separate libraries, each devoted to a different humor. The university, courting controversy, retained belief in the long discredited notion of bodily humors. Ezekiel didn't know what humor could explain the grief that Ugo seemed to feel upon witnessing the machine's sudden failure to continue recording their conversation, which concerned the ethical justification for suicide in cases of severe malaise.

The conversation could have reached a pinnacle of jurisprudential finesse, if the recorder had continued to do its job. Perhaps Ugo would have been willing, if the tape had continued to roll, to confess the strange (and probably imaginary) fungus that he believed was beginning to form over his testicular sac. So far the fungus didn't impede sexual function; if the fungus had affected Ugo's ability to make love, Ezekiel would never have turned on the cassette recorder in the first place. The realization dawned on Ezekiel that the most serious mistake he'd made, since accepting a position as librarian at an institution with only a limited hold over the popular imagination, was to bring a cassette recorder into their lives, and to insist that the magnetic device not only serve to witness domestic investigations but to supply the feeble moral pulse to a household—nay, a nation—whose humors were beginning to cry foul ball, if humors have the capacity to play the role of chatty umpire in a game of unlimited yet shadowy dimensions. The game's enigmatic nature was beyond the capacity of any blood, bile, or phlegm to adjudicate. That is why I stepped forward, despite my gout, and declared my verdict, in a voice trembling with emotion and vacillating in epoch. No listener could fix the period of my umpire-utterance, and so it had the power to revive the ailing cassette recorder, whose motor began once more to purr. I made sure to backtrack, in the narration I assembled for the cassette's sake, so that the scenes lost to posterity, thanks to the machine's temporary lapse, would now be included in the bewildering, salivating transcript that a paid secretary would compose from the cassette recording in which your interjections and rebuttals play the starring role.

The Pathos of Communication

1.

"Nobody can flee my dementia," Tom of Finland whispered to me in the aisles of a post-Soviet Walgreens. We were shopping for breakfast cereal. Dementia, manufactured by Quaker Oats, seemed a pleasurable choice, even if it didn't contain dried marshmallows, the infantile anal rage marshmallows under-girding the Transcendental Ego, at least as perceived, in the watches of the night, by the late Lucille Ball. I, too, have Ball characteristics: I want to overthrow what her co-star Vivian Vance and Immanuel Kant together called "the ambiguities of soap," a syndrome we invoke at our peril.

2.

I am in charge of revising the *World Book Encyclopedia*'s volume four, covering all subjects beginning with the letter *D*. Within my purview is *dementia*; I must rewrite its entry. Soap won't remove the fungus of non-consecutive thought; nor can I furnish the room of non-consecutiveness with appropriate furniture, such as an egg-shaped chair (The Ego as Egg) designed by a limp protégé of Ettore Sottsass, my new grandmother. I can make anyone my grandmother: I have sufficient plasticity of temperament, sufficient commitment to task-oriented and fellatio-resembling projective identification. I sat on that Sottsass-influenced chair. In its cupping embrace, I spun around, trying to remember how Ivory soap could cure every infection—or so my first pediatrician somberly declared, in the era of bacon and the March of Dimes. Better than penicillin, he claimed, was Ivory. Hew to the salves prescribed by ur-pediatricians, who sent you photographs of their naked buttocks so that you might neutralize your excessive attachment to the talc-scented hereafter. By addressing you in this elliptical manner, I reinforce the hereafter's resemblance to a bottle of "turned" Shalimar, in which you can see, floating like a dead bee, the kernel of revolutionary action I have tried to elucidate in this obedient recitation. I pay homage to Vance, to Kant, to Ball, to Sottsass, and to the anonymous pediatrician, by embracing the ridged Real—a Real whose crenellated face I caress, toward dawn, with a sphinx's rouged insistence on turning desert sand into an effigy of La Serenissima, O Venice I never visited, O Real I never violated, O soap I now dissolve.

The Sexual Translator

Sex itself he couldn't translate, but he could translate books about sex. Most books, he discovered, were about sex, whether or not the author knew it. The translator's job was to uncover what the original author could not divine. I befriended the translator late in his life, approximately ten years before his death. His funeral I didn't attend, because I took pleasure in inverting the social rules—just as I had violated the rules by befriending this august personage in the first place.

The pivotal event in our friendship concerned Mallarmé. The translator, Abel Mars, had discovered the secret key to *Divagations*, and was embarked on a translation that would reveal to the world the unsuspected sexual architecture underlying Mallarmé's sense-confounding essays, which destroyed readers while seeming to titillate them. Abel (or Abelline, as I sometimes called him, in moments of intimacy) had a fear of blue objects (vases, shirts, flowers, paintings, rugs); anything blue horrified him, perhaps because his mother had once exposed him, during a childhood attack of meningitis, to a not-yet-patented blue light, which a quack acquaintance had pushed on the family as a cure-all device for their ailing, precocious son. The blue light, which his mother had trained on his naked body as he lay on the living room carpet, had caused him to bleed from the ears; the bleeding cured his meningitis—expelling it from his body—but instilled in him a fear of anything blue. More logical it would have been if Abel had grown to fear illness itself; paradoxically, he feared not the pathogens but the anti-pathogens. He feared the cure because it came dressed in a blue aura suggesting stories he was not yet mature enough to translate, stories whose avoidance of common sense would masquerade as yet a further stain on a household already traumatized by the strange presence of a naked blue-lit boy on a living room carpet itself an unbecoming shade of orange. Orange carpets were the rage in Abel's youth, and his mother kept abreast of decor trends.

Abel's father had died in a car accident a few years before orange had crested to the summit of contemporary taste; in moments of unreason, Abel would blame orange itself for his father's death, even though orange's ascendency had postdated his father's tragic end. The network of symbolic associations linking death, illness, and color, in Abel's childhood, bore fruit in the mature translator's theories of synesthesia, principles he passed on to me, not in words, but in covert, perfumed practices. Such practices are the topic of this tale, but I am having a hard time attaining the right tone; I am avoiding any reference to the sexual action which constituted Abel's most pointed statement of translation theory. In this sexual action, which I will soon describe, Abel passed on to me a synesthetic message that undermines my capacity to reason, just as the blue light, in Abel's childhood, exorcised his meningitis while eviscerating his command of logical structures.

Abel lived in a carriage house beside a foetid yet nourishing waterway that circled the city. Nourishment entered the bloodstreams of the city's residents through a substance that the water contained, a sublimate (inhaled unconsciously) that, like an invisible fog, rose from the water and insinuated itself into the nostrils and mouths of the unsuspecting and the blessed. The water's foetid smell served as decoy; it destroyed the populace's love for a waterway on whose healing fumes rested the mental health of every child within the city limits. These fumes entered the clerestory window above Abel's study, where one evening I interrupted him, in the midst of his labors over Mallarmé, labors that sometimes took the form of naps. A Larousse dictionary was open beside him; in one sleeping hand he loosely clutched a pipe, still burning. Out the pipe came a cherry smell that slightly sickened me. I took the pipe from his hand, tamped down its foul flame, and prodded the translator awake.

I needn't bother telling you every morsel of what happened between us that evening, but don't I owe it to you, and to Iceland, to narrate the central sexual incident that dug a hole in my ratiocinative powers henceforth and undergirded my own pet theory of synesthesia, a theory I'm practicing now, as I try to make my way through this puny narrative, this parable about the co-presence of the foetid and the nourishing in every syllable a half-wit utters? I owe it to you to describe how I experienced the genitals of the translator who had cracked the code of Mallarmé's *Divagations*; I owe it to you to describe how I found myself suffused with pity for the genitals of the man, Abel Mars, who could crack a code but could not embody the enigma's solution in words that remained stable on the page. His ailment, as translator, an ailment reminiscent of his early terrified relation to the coruscating blue light a worried and quack-influenced mother trained on his precocious body, consisted in a preference for words that advertised their ambivalence by undergoing semantic and sonic changes as they seemed to sit quiescently on a page. The word *terror*, for example: how can I explain to you the sinuous behavior of the three *r*'s, as they tortured the vowels they surrounded?

That night, Abel Mars wore a silver silk bathrobe on which peacocks and alligators were embroidered in black thread; the black, loosened by red, approached purple. Abel couldn't tell that the threads were nearing purple; his infirmity had advanced to that point, a cognitive laxity analogous to the looseness of the sash binding the robe's folds together, a sash I found myself tugging, untightening and then retightening, as if wanting to exercise a power over his costume that I could not exercise over his affections. I was, to him, a mere journalist, though I prided myself on being the next great exemplar of synthesthetic sage, surpassing Abel Mars, whose theories only emerged between the lines of his translations.

To assert my status as synesthete, I undid his robe, and saw that he was wearing an undergarment that combined the traits of jock strap and festal shroud. On this strap, or shroud, feathers had been sewn, not in sweatshops, I presumed, but in ateliers staffed by acolytes of Mr. Mars. As I faced this undergarment, my own ability to distinguish imagination from reality faded; insistently I wished to uphold the actual—nonfictional—status of these undergarments, these feathers, but it was as if they were conspiring with the blue light that Abel had often described to me, the storied blue light of his childhood cure; and though I had never been subjected to extraordinary luminescences or extreme unctions, I felt Abel's undergarment— the silken reality of it—to be deliquescing into allegory, entering a foggy continuum with a blue light I'd never experienced first-hand but had only received as a story murmured to me while I lay on the day-bed of Abel Mars, afternoon after translation-saturated afternoon, as Abel caressed my young body and I caressed his older body with a dignified equanimity of regard, neither of us stinting the other or "calling the other out" (as school bullies would say) by smacking a hand or "reading the riot act," when no riot could be imagined as intruding on our adjective-soaked calm. Or do I mean gin-soaked? Those afternoons on his daybed, we weren't drinking gin; we were drinking poetry, a poetry embedded in lines of prose that, as Mallarmé dealt the tricky hand, were ostensibly chronicling a dance performance or a painter's *vernissage*.

My ability to narrate a sexual scene leaves much to be desired. All those afternoons when I lay on the daybed with Abel Mars are now blurred into one; and that erotic blur is but a prelude to the scene in question, the scene that destroyed my friendship with the translator, the scene that destroyed my relation to the language I'm now using, the scene that equips me to pontificate about the relation of actuality to metaphors, which hug each other as a desecrated chalice hugs the cherry cordial it contains.

The point of this tale is right here before you. You can touch it, smell it, taste it. Let me make it plain. I put my hand on the meek heart of the matter, the cock of Abel Mars, not for the first time. I put my hand there on this last night of our friendship, the last time I entered the carriage house beside the foetid yet nourishing waterway; I put my hand on a cock I'd often tasted on the word-stained daybed. As a gesture of conciliation and of passive-aggressive equivocation, I put my hand on the translator's cherry-tobacco penis (it smelled of cherry-tobacco, I thought, because his study was infused with that odor, and I insist on false equivalences). In this moment of reckoning, I felt like a diplomat of a country not deserving of a diplomatic corps, a country that had so spectacularly failed, on the ethical front, that it was no longer entitled to a staff of translators, peacemakers, and treaty-signers.

Now I have only twenty minutes left; in the remaining portion of this dismal, rainy afternoon, I must describe the cock of Abel Mars, and I must emphasize the foreskin's allegorical significance. His penis never emerged from its sheath; even when erect, the organ hid within the hood. Abel never reached full tumescence, because he didn't want to force his cock to break out of its protecting mantle. During our congress, that final evening in his study, the translator's penis oscillated between a state of hardness and semi-softness, a liminality for which he compensated by breathing heavily and by repeating the word *frack*, a non-signifying litany that seemed to distract him from his tenuous hold on hardness, and that seemed to reach toward a solid signification his words, on their own, could no longer achieve. "Frack, frack, frack," went the translator's pathetic litany, as he pushed his hard and then not-hard cock into mine, or onto mine, our two

cocks overlapping and competing, never melding. I hypothesized that, by repeating this death-cry or love-cry of "frack,
frack, frack," Abel was trying to intervene in the city's ecological
affairs; perhaps he wished to undo fracking, or to prevent
fracking? Perhaps he had developed a speech impediment that
turned the word *fuck* into *frack*? Perhaps *frack* was a fragment
of Victorian slang, an argot I couldn't understand? My relative
youth—I was twenty-five years younger than Abel—was a
natural resource he was trying to harvest; my dependence on
him was a pool of subterrannean oil that his organ, growing
feeble, wanted to extract. I'm telling you the truth; I have no
investment in simulation or subterfuge. The translator's cock
doesn't interest me. I wish I could be down-to-earth in
describing my indifference to Abel's phallus, but a violent
eruption of ornateness impedes my tale's delivery. That ornateness, like a ray of blue light, suffuses the room in which I'm
now writing this series of disjointed reflections on the impos-
sibility of befriending any human being who seems to possess
a power lodged in an orifice, a protuberance, or a capacity.
The protuberance—call it a cock—becomes the thing I want
to borrow, even though the librarian of the universe knows
that I never return the books, my culpable refusal robbing the
other patrons of the universal library from making use of the
orifices and protuberances that might make breathing possible. The metaphors I borrow entangle themselves in further
staircases of metaphor; the staircases, like seminal ducts, grow
thick with blocked matter. "Frack, frack, frack" means, if I
were to translate the phrase into sensible language, "I want to
borrow your embodiment." *Borrow*, here, I would translate as

destroy. Why staircases? There are no staircases in seminal ducts. There are no seminal ducts in Mallarmé. There is no foetid waterway in the library's vicinity. "There is no language to describe my fear of language," said Abel Mars, as I left his carriage house. I climbed the steps to my alcove on the fourteenth floor of the Mercantile Building, in which there will never be an elevator, not as long as my metaphors are paying the electricity bills. Later, say more about the beauties of the Mercantile Building. Say more about my alcove. Speak with more authentic regret about witnessing Abel Mars's cock, its tribulations and ambivalences. Try to render the spectacle of Abel Mars's cock with a more palpable and believable eroticism. His cock is the most exciting thing ever to happen to me in my long career of harvesting significances from forgotten phrases, so please describe his cock with language more enthusiastic, specific, and heartsore. End the description with a word referring to the appearance of a desecrated church. Describe how I ministered to Abel Mars's testicles. Be clear about how I degraded myself in the service of accuracy.

9. *[the schmatte engulfs me]*

To Be Engulfed

1.

Upon returning to a town I'd forgotten how to love, I stumbled upon a dying child. I stood outside the cottage. Uninvited, I peered through its opened window: I observed the sick boy, who lay in a box. He reminded me of a donkey I'd once pitied on a road leading to a lagoon I still fear. The child's name, I would learn later, was Arturo. His parents, impecunious villagers, had wanted him to grow up to become a famous conductor, like Arturo Toscanini, but now they were insufficiently grief-struck by their child's imminent death.

How could I claim to know the feelings of the parents? I'm no clairvoyant. My empathy skills, measured by a battery of psychological tests administered during my recent confinement, proved deficient. My only grail is tranquility—a calmness I achieve by dispensing with emotions. By forfeiting citizenship in the affective realm, I achieve Paris, my new home; I earn the right to be a parfumier on the Place Vendôme.

2.

When I return to the village, my first home, I discover the dying Arturo. The child doesn't engulf me; nor does the town, or its fishing boats, or its Sunday carnival. What engulfs me is the schmatte worn by Arturo's mother, as she leans over the box, containing a body that will soon qualify as remains. The schmatte engulfs me; I perceive its flaws and its charms; and the oscillation between *flaw* and *charm* produces a vortex in which I picture myself drowning.

When I return to Paris, I will buy a similar schmatte, from a couturier whose unconventional practice finds an unlikely locale in the smelly environs of Les Halles. My schmatte will smell of horse *contrefilets*, of veal kidneys, of calf's liver. The couturier—and her gullible customers—pretend that no foul aroma clings to the cotton. I know better. The corpse of Arturo sanctions my schmatte; I wear it, and I write these words, in his stunted honor.

Disreality

1.

At the carnival, I gave up my ice cream cone. The poor boy sitting next to me wanted the ice cream more than I wanted it. I bestowed on him the chilly treat.

As soon as the ice cream cone was out of my hands, a wave of disreality flooded over me. By relinquishing a simple pleasure, I'd become a martyr. It was within my power to purchase a second cone, but my desire for sweets had vanished.

Nor did I feel affection for the poor boy to whom I'd given my confection. I resented his melodramatic impoverishment. He looked like a Mantegna painting of a sad saint, an apostle-clown, a Jesus with the grippe. What good did my Pucci pants do me, as I sat in a carnival dominated by antiquarian stunts—men jumping from gondolas into briny waters while singing "M'appari," transposed upward for masochistic thrill?

The longer I sat reflecting on my act of charity, the more wizened I seemed to grow. I could feel my face shriveling, becoming old before my time. I took out a pocket mirror to assess my visage. In fact, I looked unchanged. No extra wrinkles. No new sag.

The boy with the ice cream cone now seemed engulfed by a trance I'd instigated. The vanilla monstrosity I'd handed him had infused him with a sense of unearned grandeur. With his eyes shut, and his hands raised, he paraded down the carnival tent's aisle. He rustled the bracelets on his arms; he gurgled and moaned. He seemed a tyrant-in-training, bound for glory or for asylum.

From my coat pocket, I extracted a pickle. Its sourness would console me for the forfeited cone. Into the experience of nibbling the pickle I would inject a novel toxin. The toxin—call it *disreality*—would permit this boy to vanish from my conscience. I had created his delusional behavior. I had fed him the fantasy of perpetual ice cream and kind strangers. I owned this carnival, but I pretended to be merely its honorary priest, hired to please mendicants.

2.

The elegant Parisian woman seated behind me had also observed the beggar-boy's perverted behavior, as he marched through an amphitheater from which the disgruntled patrons were now leaving, disgusted by the boy's noise—gruntings that he tried to pass off as melodies. A veritable tango he considered his foul plainchant, a monody with no continuo to rescue it from solipsism.

I offered the Parisienne a ride in my taxi, which took us out of the town and deposited us in a superior resort, Pro-So-Po-Peia-by-the-Sea. Here we'd be disturbed by no randy festivals, no mental illness, no delusional costermongering.

3.

The following week, when I returned to London for an emergency dermatological procedure, I read in an international newspaper that the boy, already a cause célèbre for his prestidigitations and his glossolalic raptures, had died of a tumor that no one but his great-aunt—an armchair oncologist who lived beside a lagoon, not far from Mèze, and who disclaimed any responsibility for the boy's fate—had diagnosed, with an untutored canniness I envy.

I was culpable for the gift of ice cream but not for the gift of tumor. To that boy, no poison had I consciously administered. Into the dermatological clinic I went with an unsullied conscience, my face already wrapped in gauze.

Declaration

1.

He and she had no orgasm. Talking, waxen-faced, they lay on a bed. He was topless, and she wore a glamorous dirndl.

If I were to intrude my voice, I'd mention that the hair on his chest, though sparse, earned him a place in the history—checkered, incomplete—of the *nouvelle vague.*

He and she had no interest in my voice. Omniscient and all-seeing, I lay, nearly dead, in an adjoining bedroom. Wearing a red beanie cap and a black v-neck t-shirt, I kept up a constant stream of chatter, in a Marseille dialect unknown to the psycholinguist I'd surreptitiously caressed at the cognitive science conference, last April, in Montpellier.

2.

He and she—my pet couple in the next room—sometimes tried to have an orgasm, jointly or separately. Just one orgasm, please, loud enough to disturb the dining room's sonically vigilant Limoges porcelain. Talk interfered with the couple's orgasm, as a fence interferes with poachers.

He and she discussed dirndl removal. "May I remove my dirndl?" she asked, and he replied (I could hear them through the wall), "Damn your dirndl, let me get some sleep." I translate badly.

Despite my gloom, despite my pneumonia, despite my botulism, I rose from bed and peered through the peephole connecting our chambers. She had mounted him, though both were clothed. Rub, rub, rub. How felicitous, how filmed, their motions!

Exhausted from having paid lip service to the necessity of orgasm, a destination that they had no intention of ever reaching, the couple lay back on their pallet and stared at the ceiling. I, too, returned to my inadequate mattress.

3.

Which ailment should I concentrate on? My botulism? My pneumonia? My atopicality? Sparta, I'd call this town, if we were ancient sages, but we are in France, we are modern, we have arrived at no consensus on orgasm's role in destroying the equilibrium of libertines who exhibit the devout masochism of pilgrims climbing on their knees up Rocamadour to worship at the shrine of *la Vierge noire*.

He and she are intrinsically mountain-dwellers, but they are forced to live, temporarily, in a squalid port. Pitiless sunlight reveals, to a tourist's rapacious eye, the lineaments of this harbor's grime. The contrast between opportunistic optical clarity and the port's physical decay can't rival the heaving paradoxes of my botulism and pneumonia.

4.

I survived; I became a ballet dancer. I had near-orgasms in the dressing rooms of the Palais Garnier. I forgot how to murmur in my Provençal dialect. He and she gained weight. I stopped apologizing for their sexual history. She gave me her dirndl. I wear it at night, when I'm alone, soliloquizing. Last night I spilled ketchup on the garment. Into the washing-machine went the lonely, historic dirndl, and it came out perfectly clean.

10. *[antipodes and prophecies]*

Stones and Liquor: or, Some Differences between Remorse and Regret

Clare was trying to write an essay about the difference between remorse and regret. Clare: an unusual name for a man. So be it. Clare regretted Firenze, fair city, where, stoned on edibles, he'd stumbled over the Ponte Vecchio while murmuring "This is an affluent neighborhood." A river is not a neighborhood. Clare regretted his lack of logic, a fault he couldn't remedy. He felt remorse about his inability to fix characterological defects. These flaws sprang from laziness. Too lazy to cross a bridge without eating cannabis tasties! Pretend that homoeroticism, its sandalwood aroma, was always hidden within the core of cannabis, or within the rotten pilings of an old, foul bridge, a monument he was supposed to love... Leather merchants lined the Ponte Vecchio; none of the belts or purses had appealed to Clare. He came back emptyhanded from Firenze. The memory of seeing Michelangelo's David, however, was stored like a fistula near his prostate. Clare didn't feel remorse about tourist sites unvisited. He'd paid homage to every monument, his mind afloat above the city, as if his consciousness were an orange— five oranges—on a cerise tabletop in his dead mother's remote cottage, in a town that seemed like the Paris of *Children of*

Paradise superimposed over a Latvian hamlet whose name he couldn't recall, though he'd visited it while on a research trip to study remorse's maleficent effects on the constitutions of oxen and children.

While on that Latvian adventure (shortly after his mother's death), Clare had assumed the responsibility of mentoring a nineteen-year-old fiction writer, whose short stories were the rage in nearby Riga. "Stones and Liquor" was one story that had caught the fancy of Riga's cognoscenti. Clare now remembered sitting with Hugo, the prodigy, in a café, and discussing the merits of "Stones and Liquor," especially the scene in which a vial of brandy-and-prunes hangs like a censer over the ambassador's corpse, laid out, for a wake, in the coffin, while mourning dignitaries, one by one, pass the embalmed figure, powerless now. "Be careful," Clare remembered telling Hugo; "don't allow local monsters to treat you like a harlot. Let yourself develop, without pushing your talent in whorish directions." At that moment, or so Clare recalled, Hugo's body had seemed to metamorphose. Hugo's slim head, rectilinear as a Giacometti, had seemed suddenly to puff out—not, perhaps, in actuality, but in a realm parallel to the actual, a realm that also had a basis in scientific fact and that should not be treated condescendingly by empiricists. Hugo's head, as Clare remembered, had grown dropsical and whey-colored, like Casper the Friendly Ghost; and Clare had realized that his own comment to Hugo had been the catalyst for the becoming-whey, the transposition into water-logged pallor. For instigating Hugo's deliquescence—his vaporous swelling into infantile roundness of head, a spherical gout-on-the-brain—Clare felt remorse *and* regret, the two arrows equally laced with poison. And, in a flash, it also came over Clare that he had seen a sentence suddenly appear on Hugo's now bulbous forehead: the sentence was in Latin, a dead language that his mother had enjoyed feeding him, word by word, while they watched TV together in the parlor, their heads nearly joined, as they huddled under an orange coverlet. On Hugo's forehead—in raised letters that could not be *real* letters, but must have been the artificial product of fumes inhaled from the mere phrase *brandy-and-prunes* in Hugo's story—Clare could read one Latin sentence, *Quotidie morimur et tanem nos esse aeternos putamus*, a sentence that even a remorse-addicted dolt could translate as "We die every day and therefore we consider ourselves to be immortal." Clare had cried out, "Let me lick that sentence off your blasted forehead!" And he had leaped across the table to place his fat tongue on the forehead's Braille, to remove, as if with a wet sponge, the offending, death-dealing words.

Clare regretted licking Hugo's forehead in public. Clare felt remorse that he had done such a poor job of mentoring the young fiction-writer. Clare regretted the forced haste of his departure from Latvia. Clare regretted his own exile from the forsaken parlor where he and his mother had once crouched together under an orange coverlet to watch Saturday-morning cartoons on TV. A victim of "enlightenment rationalism," as the pundits put it, Clare regretted more than anything else the presence of five oranges on the table at which he now was seated, five oranges that would have no ameliorative effect on the haze of righteousness and melancholy—misplaced righteousness, duplicitous melancholy—that Hugo, in one of his charming fits of flattery, might have called "Clare's predicament," or "Clare's cute quiddity." How not cute his quiddity was, became apparent to Clare, as he fixed his watery eyes on the five oranges, which now would be forced to fill the role of raison d'être. As if from a cave at the bottom of the Pacific Ocean, Clare could hear a plaint rise to his ear: "Pretend these words are mouthed by the hero of a 1923 silent melodrama." The film's hallucinated sprocket-holes, Clare realized, could function like the holes in pierced ears; from these sprocket-holes, Clare could hang thought-pendants, idea-jewels, made of plastic and paste. Clare could grow to adore these jewels, to worship them as if they were real. And yet Clare felt remorse for ruining Hugo's life, or for planting on his forehead a malignant seed, a tongue-germ, a licking spatula of vindictive erasure, at a café not twenty miles from Riga—a slurping gesture that Clare performed in a perverted attempt to make *not happen* a sentence that had already happened.

A Few Don'ts about Yellow Wallpaper

The wallpaper's polka dots may have resembled 8mm film sprockets, but he had promised himself not to get distracted. Were he to reread Charlotte Perkins Gilman's "The Yellow Wallpaper," he'd discover a link between its heroine's madness and his own. However, he didn't want to revisit a tragic book. Ten years had passed since the last perusal. That elapsed decade made him more handsome, not less. Shouldn't, by now, I tell you his name? Ted Dallesandro. A long last name stops conversation cold.

Ten years ago, Ted had completed his dissertation about "The Yellow Wallpaper." This morning, he woke to a distressing phone call from his alma mater's registrar. Turns out that Ted had made a fatal formatting error. He'd used endnotes instead of footnotes. A new librarian was now in charge of reviewing past dissertations to ascertain if they complied with current bibliographic regulations. This librarian disliked Ted's formatting, and insisted that Ted retype the dissertation, this time using footnotes. Slow were the wheels of Ted's cognition, as he listened to the registrar explain the new edict.

I can't speed up Ted's cognitive wheels, much as I try. But I can describe Ted Dallesandro's appearance, and that information might improve your mood.

In the years between the composition of *A Few Don'ts about Yellow Wallpaper* and this morning's phone call from the abusive registrar, Ted's resemblance to a young Nicolas Cage had given way to a resemblance to Jean-Luc Godard at forty. Sadness and a sense of forfeited opportunities had etched fine lines in Ted Dallesandro's countenance. Ted's eyes moved slowly across the room; they landed on objects—ottoman, pitcher, lamp, conch shell—with neutrality and a slight rebuke. To see an object is to rebuke it for not providing more love, more conversation—but only the insane would expect a conch shell to explain and gossip. Ted may want "dish"—palaver—from the conch, but the conch won't kibitz.

Ted, though not a load-bearing element in this tale, was trying to explain, to the unseen cinematographer, the meaning of tragedy. The "unseen cinematographer" was a phrase that Ted and his mother had employed, together, in their table talk, when he was first studying modernist fiction at the university now questioning, ex post facto, the legitimacy of his Ph.D. Of course Ted had lived with his mother while studying for his Ph.D.; I don't have time, this morning, to explain the folds and undulations of the Ted/mother nexus, and the beverages associated with that nexus. Ted and his mother treated this "unseen cinematographer" as a fall guy—a punching bag, invisible and comic, in the kitchen, where Ted and his mother would sit, making crescent rolls and doing crossword puzzles.

The night before the university's belligerent registrar had telephoned, Ted had returned from Mexico City; he'd spent most of his time there cruising the bookstores, looking for psychoanalytic stimulation. Could he find, in a bookstore, a text that would undo his paralysis? Even a cookbook could loosen a cathexis, if the index were thorough. Hardly limited to a bookstore's psychology section were the possible catalysts of cure, according to Ted's nimble method of bibliomancy, a latter-day *Sortes Vergilianae*—whereby a phrase in an auto-repair manual, spotted in a back-alley bookstore stumbled upon while drunkenly wandering, could bring about a revolution in Ted's poorly-sorted mental filing-cabinet, the folders unlabeled and bug-infested. On this foray to Mexico City, Ted had discovered a pamphlet about wallpaper removal and replacement, a short, self-published essay, so curious and illogical in its argumentation, so bereft of illustrations, that he'd suddenly surmised that the death of a pop star (by drug overdose) and the interpretation of a modernist classic (by a poseur) were parallel disasters.

To fail was one prohibition—one "don't"—that yellow wallpaper, according to Ted, offered a world hungry for advice. But the world had reason to question Ted, to say "I'm confused." World had reason to say, "Should I fail or succeed? Which path does yellow wallpaper advise?" The fact that Ezra Pound once wrote a bossy but inspiring essay entitled "A Few Don'ts by an Imagiste" disgusted Ted, and delighted his mother, for whom modernism was like marmite, a sentimental favorite.

Why should world listen to yellow wallpaper? Simply because Ted looked like Godard at forty, and formerly resembled

Cage? In whose eyes was the resemblance to Godard, or to Cage, a boon? In whose eyes was the resemblance a liability? The eyes of the unseen cinematographer, or of Ted's mother? Ted's mother had good reason to resent world for its intrusive questions, its hunger for placebo-advice. Ted's mother, Inghilterra Dallesandro, had eschewed wallpaper, in an act of connoisseurship that had the power, even this morning, to fill Ted with longing and remorse. No wallpaper in Inghilterra's kitchen. No wallpaper in Inghilterra's bedroom, or in Ted's. No unseen cinematographer. A vast silence, as in a bookstore after closing hour, descended upon Ted's capacity to envision his future. The future, like a nude restaurant before it had decided to become nude, lay open to the prospect of liberation but couldn't find the pamphlet that explained how to operate liberation's emergency exits, how to find liberation's fallout shelters, how to liquidate liberation when its openness to wonder had ceased.

Pink Eye (A Family Romance)

This morning I woke up with pink eye, which will prevent me from consummating my relationship with Nellie. A naked man on the roof across the street is performing yoga moves. I'm jealous of his athleticism, ashamed of my pink eye, and sad about failing to please Nellie, to whom I owe a definition of tragedy. We are classmates in a night-school seminar, "The Tragic Sense of Life," in which we are watching *Berlin Alexanderplatz*, *The Conformist*, *Salò*, and other films that treat moral rot as elixir.

Back to Nellie, and to the dreams I left behind, in her capacious houseboat, the last time I visited. Nellie's bedroom had pink walls, each pocked (like malfunctioning stucco) with sponge-holes. Can stucco malfunction? Or is stucco always competent? I touched Nellie's curly hair, a bundle, like Streisand's 'fro in *A Star Is Born*. Remarkably artificial was Nellie's hair, and I abetted its stiffness by commenting on it. Nellie despised my susceptibility to pink eye; no logical relation obtained between pink eye and fulsomeness, though these character flaws made me ineligible for houseboat-ownership.

Strange Amsterdam we sought nourishment from, in night school! "The splendor of the crepuscular," our instructor murmured, hoping to feed us knowledge of the tragic sense of life, which we could find only in the microtonal differences between apples and aporia—the hole of unknowing, where our conversation foundered, leaving us uncertain about whether we could make a living in a city inhospitable to dream-prone émigrés.

Could I do a better job of explaining the differences between apples and aporia? First I must rid myself of the delusion that Nellie wants to consummate our relationship. Her nose is larger than mine; we both have elongated nostrils, and bumps at the bridge, the nose's climax, where it divides the solemn eyes. "I don't want you to dwell exclusively in dreams," Nellie said, last night, taking a cue from our "tragic-sense-of-life" instructor, who also had derided my reliance on somnambulism. We composed a family—Nellie, the instructor, and I. This morning I want to erase the instructor, to remove her from Amsterdam's consciousness. I want to evict Nellie from her hazardous houseboat. I want to cure my pink eye. Paradoxically I love my pink eye and I want Nellie to live forever cloistered in her flunky bedroom. The instructor, a Borges nut, has threatened to schedule a tête-à-tête tragic-sense-of-life tutorial breakfast with Nellie. And therefore I must erase the instructor.

Before erasing the instructor, I should tell you her name, and give you a sense of why she deserves erasure. She is the goddaughter of Dino De Laurentiis, a noble lineage that may mean nothing to you; I pity you for not caring about the instructor's pedigree. You, too, are in danger of erasure, unless you work up some emotional response to the instructor's natal link to a great producer, whose role in bringing *Nights of Cabiria* to the world is tantamount to a hale dose of random nudity, in my estimation.

The instructor, Renata Pawlowski—ill-paid, devoted, mercurial, half-Italian and half-Polish—runs the philosophic wing of Amsterdam's greatest night-school, and claims to be a descendant of Anna Pavlova. Renata teaches in the evening, and models during the day. Her career as mannequin offers her plenty of leisure time for studying philosophy and translating Borges.

"Sólo una cosa no hay. Es el olvido." So Renata begins every evening's seminar—with a recitation from Borges, always the same poem. Renata wants to establish oblivion as our nocturnal habitat, the place where we can gather and cuddle, where we can tenderly violate each other's thresholds, under the guise of tragedy-sourcing, trying to find where the tragic river begins, in what corner of consciousness, perhaps an underground well, its cold unseen water as remote from practicality as the flesh-tone in Ingres's *La Source*, a painting of a nude woman who resembles me, though I, a Daniel, am not Daniela, and am not as round-figured and clear-skinned as the Ingres divinity. Oblivion is not my last name. My last name is Archetechno, a name I adopted to replace my patronym, Cohen.

I can't justify my presence in Amsterdam, when business in Tel Aviv awaits my attention. My funds are zilch. I seem to be depicting Nellie as a sex-fiend, but her erotic life is opaque to me, and beyond the reach of this narrative. Our romance consists of memorized abstractions, mazes, antipodes and prophecies. This story's destructive powers, and its diseased pinkness, know no bounds. Try to imagine a world in which the Nazis had never come to power. Try to imagine a world without *Nights of Cabiria*. Try to imagine Renata's displeasure at my caracoles, and her desire for Nellie to stop relying on me as study-partner and large-nosed doppelgänger-confidant. Take this much-touted "tragic sense of life" and nibble it, as if it were a ginger snap. Be nourished by the contradictions, and don't drag your dirty hands on my clean pink stucco bedroom wall.

On my wall, a coral-pink rectangle nests inside a blush square. The pallor of the background pink is not the antidote to your suffering. Degrees of invisibility and inaudibility please only the punitive yet dedicated schoolteacher. As she paces the seminar room, I can hear the click-click-click of her melancholy heels, an aural stimulation I must now disavow. No more sweet sounds for me. No more pablum ambiguities. From now on, just the hard tack of perpetual flight—fleeing from the Renata/Nellie predicaments, the Amsterdam/Tel Aviv conundrums, the *Cabiria/Alexanderplatz* amnesias, the unflattering mirror in which I scrutinize my pink eye.

On Not Being Able to Paint

The painter and I stood beside our friend Pascal on a hotel atrium's balcony. A mercantile convention (concerning potted meats) surrounded us and justified our presence here at the Ritz, in a depressed town not deserving a fancy hotel.

The painter became a murderer by pushing our friend Pascal over the balcony. Pascal surrendered passively to the painter's assault; it came as no surprise. The painter and I had tired of Pascal's conversation. Pascal couldn't transcend potted meats; any other subject of discussion failed to excite him.

The painter pushed Pascal over the balcony with a sudden thrust—as if in a bench-press maneuver calculated to impress a future lover. Pascal had never intended to be a painter; he was content to dwell within the realm of potted meats. Therefore it seemed gratuitous for the painter to destroy Pascal, who represented no competition.

I thought that I was the only person who saw the painter push Pascal over the balcony; therefore, this cruel act seemed abstract, a mere speculation, not a crime.

Down and down I could see Pascal fall, but in a quick unstable blur, the man seeming half pebble and half person, a bundle of unrelated limbs. I could see Pascal's integumental fibers collapse and declare themselves bogus, the "Pascal" illusion decomposing in that blurry moment of his fall downward to the atrium's floor.

Where Pascal fell, a circle of observers quickly gathered. I stepped back from visibility. From below, observers could perhaps see the painter, who still stood gloating at the balcony's edge; but I was now unseeable.

"You think you're just a porgy swimming in the garden of Eden," the painter said to me. "You think you're a small-town Macbeth, with his puny soliloquies and his daydreams. No comment on your so-called innocence."

Could I refuse responsibility for Pascal's fall? The painter leaned against me. I must not let him touch me, despite my month-long attempt to seduce him, an attempt culminating at this potted-meat convention.

Against my will, he grabbed me in a long, sticky, Judas hug. I could feel our amoral consanguinity surround me, like a soiled cape.

The painter had let go of me by the time the observers from the atrium had ascended by elevator to our aerie. I expected tough cross-examination, but the ringleader of the witnesses, a stout man who introduced himself as Mr. Mud (he spoke with a thick German accent), asked the painter, with admirable gentleness, about his recent *vernissage*. Clearly, Mr. Mud would only gradually make his inquisitional way toward the murder.

How, though, did I know that Pascal was dead? Perhaps he had survived the fall. I looked down and saw the Pascal-body surrounded by a nimbus of splatter. Pascal's so-called limbs lay in a starfish pattern around him; they seemed, these flesh-sticks, to be still connected to his trunk, but they resembled spokes from a dismembered bicycle wheel or a wind-destroyed umbrella.

"That man must have insulted you," Mr. Mud assured the painter. "I imagine that's why you pushed him over the balcony." Mr. Mud chuckled. "People at conventions behave strangely. Just this morning a sausage vendor insulted me when I asked him about fat ratios. There's no end to the derision surrounding us, and we sometimes need to take action. Sometimes it's not enough to put up with insult and expect people to mind their manners. Sometimes we need to push."

The painter cracked his knuckles; the sound was pleasant yet repellent.

Replying to Mr. Mud, the painter said, "Ten years ago, I'd stopped painting. I couldn't lift a brush or a palette knife. I no longer saw shapes when I woke—inchoate forms beckoning me to represent them. During that period, I met Pascal. Ten years later, I see him again, and he repeats to me the exact same words he'd said ten years ago."

"What were those words?" asked Mr. Mud, politely, his fingers digging in his ears for wax.

"*Frugal muse, frugal muse,*" said the painter. "A plainsong. *Frugal muse, frugal muse.* Pascal wasn't a painter. Pascal wasn't educated. He was a meat man, period. But we drank at the same bar, and I'd grown to depend on his grunting witticisms and half-baked nonsense-chants. One night it was *ape in Eden, ape in Eden.* I'm drinking my vodka, and Pascal is repeating *ape in Eden, ape in Eden,* which I begin to hear as *happen Eden,* or *Eden is once again happening*. Eden returns to me—the paradise of wanting to paint—because this drunk fool murmurs *ape in Eden* while he fondles my leg, right there at the crowded bar."

"Was Pascal unclothed?" asked Mr. Mud.

"No," the painter said. "Pascal was fully dressed, but his trousers were loose, and he didn't wear underwear, so I could feel his trusty business, offering itself to me. A fool's equipment he had, and I accepted it."

"Let's return to *frugal muse*," offered Mr. Mud, whose role was not simply prosecution and investigation, but continuity. I noticed bits of dried food affixed to Mr. Mud's handlebar mustache.

The painter replied, "*Frugal muse* was what Pascal said, when I saw him here today, for the first time in ten years. "

"Was that an insult?" asked Mr. Mud.

"I resented Pascal for thinking that my muse had been parsimonious."

"Frugality doesn't necessarily mean crappiness," I whispered to the painter, but softly enough that Mr. Mud couldn't hear.

"And if *frugal muse* seemed an insult," Mr. Mud said, with an unctuous smile, "then you were justified in pushing that man over the balcony. Or at least you'd believed yourself justified."

"No," said the painter. "It was a momentary impulse I now regret." The painter walked back to the balcony's edge and looked down. "Poor Pascal, wrecked there on the Ritz floor. I hadn't meant to destroy him."

"I'll need to call the hotel police," said Mr. Mud, "though I'm sure they'll understand your position."

"Frugal muse," I said, loudly enough for Mr. Mud and the painter to hear. Bovine, they gaped at me. Suddenly I realized that Mr. Mud and the painter both had jowls and blood-shot eyes.

The skylight of the Ritz atrium opened, and a flock of birds entered, loudly cawing.

"Demanding birds," said Mr. Mud, shading his eyes from the bright sunlight admitted by the opened ceiling, a gash disturbing its surface.

I wanted to transcend causality and punishment, and these birds seemed one serendipitous answer, if I could learn to translate their incoherent but precisely patterned cries.

I took the elevator downstairs to look at Pascal's body. The crowd had dispersed. Remaining in the downstairs lobby were bellhops, concierge, receptionists, and a few stray convention-attendees, each wearing a plastic nametag. One group of visitors stood in front of a vitrine that contained either hotel souvenirs or jewels.

What I saw in the place where I'd expected to find Pascal's body is beyond my capacity to describe.

The painter took me, that evening, to a decent restaurant, where I ordered *cacio e pepe*. The strands of spaghetti were clustered within a Parmesan basket—encrusted cheese, hardened to form a fist-sized enclosure, in which the coiling pasta could rest, like a wig overflowing its wig-box. The painter ordered fried artichokes. He complained that the chef had not isolated the edible hearts, but had included, on the plate, huge chunks of indigestible matter.

The Artist's Methods

My technique, as an artist, was to photograph another person's novel—page by page—with a clumsy, large, outdated Polaroid camera. I feared that my latest project, a blow-by-blow photographic reproduction of *Ensemble Piece* (a novel about an Aixois cinematographer having an affair with a working-class boy from East London), would get me in trouble with the courts. I'd always approached plagiarism—the specter of it—with lighthearted indifference. But a scapegoating chill had descended over the artistic community, and all acts of imitation were now verboten.

In the novel *Ensemble Piece*, the cinematographer behaved with a paradoxically cruel protectiveness toward his protégé, an unkempt, overweight, needy boy, often tearful, who had a behavioral condition that the novelist described as mild autism, though I dispute the diagnosis. I photographed the pages of *Ensemble Piece* without changing its language, though I would have liked to improve its diction and syntax. *Ensemble Piece*—the original potboiler, not my photograph of it—included (as appendices) 45-rpm records of torch songs performed by women who looked like Dusty Springfield but who didn't have major reputations.

I'd found the saga *Ensemble Piece* in the attic of a New England house where I'd spent Halloween. That evening, after the trick-or-treaters had dispersed, and the vandals and mauraders had finished their dirty work, I'd read the romance while crouched on the attic floor, my bare knees grinding into the seamed, splintery floorboards. The novel told the story of a man who spied on the erotic doings of a younger man. Here was a saga I could imagine photographing, not for profit, but for love of the clear, cloudless moods that came from copying.

Weeks later, I began my saga of copying—page by page, my stomach grumbling, as if I were hungry for the product, not the process. Out curled one Polaroid after another from my hungry, criminal machine. By photographing the novel, I begged it to remain unfinished. And yet it had been published years ago, and its author was no doubt dead. Marjorie Wilcox Braunweig. Look her up, you won't find a trace of her. She might once have been a household name. In the author photo, she resembled Sylvia Plath. Did Braunweig also contribute, as uncredited chorister, to the 45-rpm records included as appendices?

I sat on a speeding train—traveling from a Bavarian village in Pennsylvania to a Roman town in Ulster County. Walking down the aisle toward me was a young man, Valentin, formerly my apprentice. Coarse-featured, with lips thickened by nervous self-biting, Valentin carried a full ashtray; I sensed that he planned to empty it on my lap. The ashtray along its rim had the indentations I adore, the finger-sized clefts in which a cigarette, *in medias res*, could rest, with the melancholy that only an unfinished cigarette has the effrontery to epitomize.

Had I the power to alter the novel I was photographing—had I the power to change the words of Braunweig's *Ensemble Piece*—I'd have ended with that ashtray, and with the violence of lip-bitten Valentin spilling ashes on my lap. The ashes and the ashtray symbolized something momentous—perhaps the graves, in Europe and South America, of my ancestors; perhaps my own callousness and amorality; perhaps my devotion to mourning, and the amount of my life I'd wasted in fruitless, circling obsequies; or perhaps my cruelty to this troubled boy-man, this naïve golem, approaching me with his ashtray, on a train moving erratically and bumpily across an industry-scarred landscape impossible to see clearly through the filthy windows. I felt an illicit, opportunistic surge of happiness, because I knew—or vainly hoped—that I could end my photographed novel with a scene involving this ashtray.

Valentin's nose, as usual, was running; he couldn't wipe it, because he was holding the ashtray. The snot ran down toward his lip, in a not unattractive runnel. When Valentin had been my apprentice, I'd taken nude photographs of him with a Polaroid camera; his apprenticeship had included nudity, for which I now had reason to feel shame and regret, although the cultural organization that had employed me and had paid Valentin's salary was an experimental enterprise known for its devotion to states of undress. No secret to the world was our traffic in nudity, our researches in nude living, nude intellection, nude commerce, nude melancholy. As part of our organization's work, I'd taken photographs of Valentin and had wanted to use them as illustrations in a novel I was photographing, but I didn't have the right to add photographs to a novel whose given, unalterable surface was already composed of images.

After Valentin had ceased to be my apprentice, I'd continued to take nude photographs of him, despite his afflictions and his growing unsightliness. By giving me the ashtray, a peace offering, he meant to honor and to appease me, and yet I interpreted his kind gesture as insult, as proof of mental illness, as token of his irremediable criminality. He seemed to treat the ashtray as a musical instrument—a thumb piano or zither. The ashtray's music was rudimentary and therefore violent. By approaching me, with a brazenness that violated the train's covenant and our puppet-dictatorship's protocols, Valentin seemed to offer the ashtray as a prediction of what I would become after he'd destroyed me. (His Vesuvius-bright gaze made clear that he intended to slay me by the end of our journey.) The ashes, in the round and open dish, were the aesthetic distillate of everything I'd tried to accomplish in my painstaking art.

Suddenly he toppled—upended—the tray and let the ashes fall onto my lap. I was wearing off-white corduroy trousers, their Floridian cotton too thin for November. The ashes, when I tried to brush them off my trousers, became embedded in the corrugations. The more I rubbed the ashes, trying to remove them from my pants, the deeper they sequestered themselves between the grooves.

Two uniformed policemen came down the aisle and handcuffed my young friend, the swollen-lipped Valentin, and took him away. I watched his body recede, along the aisle's vanishing point. Valentin's shirt was untucked, the tail torn and soiled.

And I remembered our hour of swordplay together, when we'd pretended to be gladiators, a year ago, on the organization's premises. I, too, had consented to be photographed by a resident artist; I, too, had donned a loincloth and allowed the jack-of-all-trades rehearsal pianist to smear my body with mineral oil.

Valentin's trial, mock or real, would be speedy. Perhaps the state would choose to omit a trial, and impose sentence and imprisonment without due process. We lived under a puppet dictatorship, and the trains were the new government's central gathering-places and conduits, and hence the country's most vigilantly monitored spaces. If I chose to visit Valentin in prison, I'd bring my Polaroid camera and photograph his face in confinement. Imprisonment would bring him closer to his final ripening, a fruition that I would oversee. Inwardly I gloated, as I mulled over the morbid paradox that the state will have locked up Valentin while leaving me free to photograph and create copy-novels, exact replications of originals found in attics, dumpsters, and Salvation Army racks.

I'm describing Valentin's fruition in a blurred, abstract fashion, to protect his privacy. He wouldn't want me to reveal the explicit, embarrassing details of that bodily ceremony we agree to call his "final ripening," a scene I don't have the right to linger over in phrases calculated to titillate.

"Valentin," I'll say to him, when I visit him in prison, "tell me the story of the ashtray." Valentin's grandmother will be visiting at the same time. She, too, will want to hear the ashtray saga. The scheme of his punishment requires that Valentin must do our bidding, and repeat a tale he doesn't understand. I could heal Valentin by explaining the ashtray. I could appeal his sentence. Instead, I repeat it. Loincloth or not, I profit from obfuscation. Therein lies my amorality. I haven't laundered the ash-stained cords, cerements fouled by Valentin's lapse.

In the next chapter, I will help Valentin escape from prison. We will overthrow the government, in our own paltry fashion. We will take a boat to an unnameable island and start a new nude organization, of which Valentin will be executive director. Gulls and cormorants will serve on the board of trustees.

11. *[oddments cribbed from funerals]*

Sebald Sandwich

W. G. Sebald had a more complicated life than most readers realize. He spent the summer of 1985 in Oklahoma City, where he ate, every noon, at a modest café that I recently visited. I ordered a tongue-with-horseradish-sauce sandwich also called, on the menu, a "Sebald sandwich." My waitress brought me an indiscriminate platter of left-over sandwiches: "I'll give you this whole tray for ten bucks," she said. I stared at the unimpressive array; I was chagrined to see that the sandwiches were on bagels, not regular bread. I told the waitress, in a tone whose uncharitableness now gives me shame to remember, "I don't want these tawdry leftovers. I want a freshly-made Sebald sandwich." From among the debris on the platter, the waitress fished out a pale approximation of a Sebald sandwich and handed it to me. I repeated my insulting demand: "I don't want an ersatz version on a skimpy bagel. I ordered a normal Sebald sandwich." After great delay, and a series of further miscommunications and disappointments, which it would be tedious to describe, I received my long-awaited Sebald sandwich. Upon finishing it, I told the harried, grumpy waitress, "Sebald was a theater person. Theater people like to eat at overpriced cafeterias. Theater people glorify these watering holes, which then become tourist attractions, like Sardi's. I distrust any restaurant that becomes a cult locale." The waitress was grumpy, but she was also talented and beautiful. She looked exactly like a young Roberta Flack, famous for "Killing Me Softly with His Song."

Tortoise

Our plane landed in Alabama, though we first thought we'd landed in Michigan.

A country singer (lesbian, skinny) was signing books on a porch. She had frizzy hair, and a big fan base.

I wandered away from the airplane. Eventually I'd return to the airplane, to finish the flight (its final destination was San Francisco).

In my wanderings, I spied a tortoise. It, too, was an émigré from the airplane.

The tortoise barely qualified as a tortoise. Call it an embryonic approximation.

I befriended the embryo.

The quasi-tortoise found a cigarette butt. The quasi-tortoise maneuvered its body and mouth to surround the lit butt.

I marveled at the tortoise's ingenuity; but was smoking good for the tortoise's health? The butt was almost as big as the tortoise's entire body.

Gradually the tortoise changed its mind about that behavior, and assumed upright identity, near a bus stop.

The tortoise, once it had achieved freestanding vertical status, resembled a rock star from the 1970s, a has-been. But this rock star was also sexually commanding—a guy with intimidating swagger.

My fears that a car would run over the tortoise diminished. At this point in the story, my relation to the now-upright tortoise-star was subservient. I feared that the upright tortoise-star would harass me for being insufficiently masculine, or for being insufficiently independent.

Independence, however, was a dubious concept, highly ideological. And no one in Alabama—if, indeed, we were in Alabama, and not Michigan—could assist me in decoding sovereignty's malign undercurrents.

Later, after my consciousness had shut down, the tortoise reappeared, but its personality had changed, as had mine. I can't define for you those changes, because a new vision has overtaken this waking nightmare that pundits call a nation. I saw a father carrying a baby on his shoulders. The father was dancing, solo, by a barren apple tree. The baby was nominally part of the dance, but only as a passive passenger, riding on the prime mover's shoulders. I remember the flavor of that tree's apples, before it had ceased to produce fruit. The apples had the library-like richness of aged port—moldering paper, fire-places, dust. I remember those apples, scattered like a spangled skirt around the tree's base. So abundant were the apples, we left them on the ground to rot. We regret the rot, but not the abundance.

The King of Nevada

With utmost quickness I am required to write a résumé for the king of Nevada.

But what if the king of Nevada has not accomplished anything, and there will be nothing to put on his résumé?

Should I try to get a job with the king of Colorado, instead?

Where are the job listings?

Meanwhile I'm stuck with the king of Nevada.

What if I make up credentials, and the media discover my fraudulence, and someone sues the king of Nevada for fraud?

Do I love the king of Nevada, or am I simply in his employ?

I visited Nevada only once; I marveled at Reno's factories, its makeup warehouses, where canisters of lip gloss were stored—acres of gloss, badly lit, in buildings no one visited or tended.

Despite my non-attachment to Nevada, I make my living by doing errands for Nevada's lame-duck king. The king doesn't live in Nevada, though ostensibly he rules its populace.

The king has few supporters, no queen, no retinue, no press agent. His staff has dwindled to three: a cook, a maid, and me.

And I am part-time!

When the king knocks on my cubicle's partition—in ten minutes—I will hand him whatever sheaf of lies I can put together on his sordid, defunct behalf.

The king retains crown jewels, but they are paste—composed of perishable nutmeats, and of oddments cribbed from funerals the royal family has crashed.

Funerals are a little-known source of harvest for prospectors in search of oddments for later assembly into crown jewels.

No one ever doubted the ingenuity of the royal family, even the king, whom some commentators have called "legally brain-dead" (others have called him a "maraschino-style nonpareil, useless and red and cosseted").

The king is not brain-dead; this morning, I waited on him at table, and his conversation had the usual inconsequential nimbleness, leaping from allusions to Wimbledon (or its Nevada equivalent—forgive me for not remembering the Nevada equivalent to Wimbledon!) to diatribes against Alla Nazimova, whose *Salomé*, filmed in Las Vegas, enthralled the queen mother, long ago, when the queen mother was alive and capable of being enthralled by "pictures."

My resemblance to the queen mother—jowls, and a tiara of white curls around the brow—may give the king some comfort, when he reviews, late at night, his dwindling estate, his eyelids heavy, as mine are heavy now, narcotized by dreams of crudités—radishes I loved when, as a boy, I walked the land with Father, and we inspected our fecund domain. Sometimes, in a moment of ecstatic risk, Father would reach his hand directly to the ground, pull up a radish, and thrust it at me. I'd eat the radish without wiping it off first. Dirt cincturing the radish seemed a premonition of the service I would end up doing (a part-time thralldom, not particularly helpful) for a king whose dominion has all the authority of a flea market in the rain, on the outskirts of Paris, after the city has been bombed to smithereens, and the remaining populace is no longer in the mood to shop for bruised tokens of aftermath— or should I simply say "junk"?

His Husband

His husband got fired.

His husband, beaky, formerly worked in fashion.

I met his husband at the hospital, in the dermatology clinic waiting room.

His husband was yelling at the receptionist.

His husband doesn't like me because I am also beaky and therefore represent a threat. I am a woman, but I am beaky. My beakiness intrudes on his husband's territory. About his beakiness, his husband feels an imperialist's sense of manifest destiny. In an earlier era, "conquer the colonies for the sake of my beakiness" might have been his husband's motto.

I haven't defined beakiness.

Beakiness involves abruptness of nose and chin—a collaborative vendetta waged by nose and chin against the surrounding atmosphere, which may include other patients in the dermatology clinic waiting room.

I work in fashion, but in a finer house than his husband's.

My house is not as important as Chanel, but my house is not invisible.

I could waste time here belaboring the visible complexities

of my house, but the ushers will kick me out before I finish my explanations.

If I were to compare his husband to a fruit, I would choose persimmon. His husband looks bruised, like a specialty item that ordinary shoppers would avoid.

My boss broke her leg on Monday. Today, Thursday, my boss is still taking Percocet, and complains loudly about her pain.

If I were to compare my boss to a piece of fruit, I would choose honeydew melon. Although she is my boss, and therefore supposedly an authority, her behavior is reprehensibly honied—or so I have heard the elders murmur in their hushed, illicit convocations.

At my desk, where I sit, writing this diatribe, I can see, out a window, an atrium, where the workers at this fashion house gather at noon to hear their orders.

His husband, formerly a man who gave orders, will use up his severance package, and then will never find another job, because he is beaky.

Though I, too, am beaky, my position at this house is sufficiently subordinate that my angular mien isn't held against me. It alienates no one. Nor does it attract attention. My beakiness, like Rachel Carson's *Silent Spring*, is a cry that will go unheard, whether in atrium or in Congress.

You might argue that *Silent Spring* gave birth to the ecology movement. But you have no place in this diatribe; and with this final sentence I eject you forever from the inner sanctum of my unhusbanded consciousness.

12. *[keep vaudeville vague]*

Variety Springs

My name is Siegfried Kracauer. (Not the famous thinker.)

Everything I do is legal. My accountability rating is high. I see patients for a form of "talk therapy" that includes touching. Licensed, I charge $80 an hour. Rents are cheap in Variety Springs.

I had a brief acting career—commercials, soaps, summer stock. I lack a middle initial.

I'm five foot five. That's small, for a masseur. It's difficult for me to get leverage.

Current favorites: Aeneas, Killer 69. Patients, protégés, friends.

My mother used to say, "You have no sense of humor!"

What stern, authoritarian handwriting I have! Like a religious studies scholar. Which religion?

*

I'm a Marxist, sexually speaking. I'm single. I discombobulate inherited structures.

I'll undergo this self-analysis for five months.

Momentarily my suicidal tendencies and my hypomania have abated.

*

My treatment room: purple velvet tacked to its walls. A small electric waterfall, always in motion: white noise machine. Massage table. Two Eames chairs.

My curly red hair: attractive feature. Not dyed. I don't look like a freak. My patients trust me.

Just now I pressed my ear to the floor to hear the shouting and smacking (spanking sessions) in my downstairs neighbor's apartment: Benjamin Levi, sadist.

Once, he told me, "Don't jab my balls with your umbrella."

I wasn't holding an umbrella.

*

During sessions, I must sometimes assume a mime's silence, to allow the patient's verbiage to fill the room.

Smack smack again resounds Benjamin Levi's hand on some navvy's buttocks.

*

Here's my all-purpose eulogy.

Max, drug dealer in the house next door, was found dead—OD—in his kitchen. Body left there to rot for a half-week before discovery. Messianic gaze, nimble on his dirty-sandaled feet: I never forget a dead man, even if we weren't close. Minor acquaintances who die—their disappearances prove most wounding. Where's the pockmarked woman with flipflops—the one I'd see daily, holding her ratty pooch, in the park? Heart failure?

*

Variety Springs, New York: small town with a big-city density. High percentage of gays. Loose morals. History of countenanced prostitution. Absence of police action. High percentage of Jews. One orthodox *shul*. Not my scene. Many of my patients are Jews: fine with me.

Aeneas owns a used CD and record shop, Miracle Music. For dinner: chicken legs. Or thighs?

*

Future topics: my psychiatric training (sketchy); sadness of being an only child; my libertarian philosophy; my illustrious namesake, Siegfried Kracauer.

*

I stepped into Miracle Music, empty of customers. Aeneas did my astrological chart. My "Sun Q" is in Sagittarius, "by ecliptic," Aeneas says, which explains my cheerfulness. My S is "in Scorpio H," which means, says Aeneas, that I am secretive, reclusive, and easily hurt by imagined or actual rebuffs.

I jumble chakras.

Aeneas is thirty years old, 163 pounds, from Lisbon. Some days his voice usurps mine.

"Have you visited Karl Marx's birthplace in Trier, the oldest town in Germany?" Aeneas asked me, after doing my chart.

Massaging his feet in our last session, I noticed incipient hammer toe, right foot.

His brother has cerebral palsy. Aeneas feels guilty for pursuing an independent existence in Variety Springs, thousands of miles from Baton Rouge, where his brother and their widowed mother live together. After Aeneas's father died, the family, seeking opportunity and amnesia, emigrated from Lisbon to Louisiana. Aeneas's mother loves a tornado sidetracked and dissipated before it can lay waste to the city, as the inept Cassandras of the weather channel had foretold.

O Aeneas, your *horror vacui* is only exceeded by my own.

Hair patch above Aeneas's butt: sweat marks the spot.

Aeneas told me that his father's spirit, postmortem, overtook the son's body and ruled it for weeks. A turquoise glow outlined the boy's torso. Eventually the aura faded and the family left Lisbon.

My lot: *unlikeability*. Quoth Benjamin Levi, downstairs. Why trust a sadist? Because he has freckled shoulders: visible in tank tops.

*

Death of Jed, owner of Tunnel Traffic Books, in Variety Springs. I never deeply cared for him, though he could forecast my reading tastes. Jed vanishes: in response, go to the pharmacy for a refill. Adelle, druggist, who looks like Sylvia Miles in *Midnight Cowboy*, says, "Siegfried, take these pills with food." She forgives in me the retrograde dreamer who chooses what Soviets call "inner exile" over the pioneer rigors of nation-building.

I am communist at heart. Pink, I am stilted in verbal expression, nasally clogged. I am a peony somewhere between white and red.

Two o'clock appointment with Stavros. A newish patient. Aeneas's longtime lover, friend from childhood. So far it's been mostly talk. Today we might proceed to lightweight erotic healing. His nonverbal connection skills (eye contact) are excellent, but his speech is disorganized, and he shows avolitional tendencies—unwillingness to open the treatment-room door by himself, unwillingness to call the dentist to make an appointment to clean his decaying teeth. I will tell Stavros, when the session begins, as I tell each of my clients, "Be aware of what you want from me, and why you want it, and from whom in the past you have wanted the same."

*

A characteristic of Stavros's speech is overelaborateness. In today's session, he said, "My childhood friend's father, Mr. Petrucci, drove ninety miles an hour on the highway through Baton Rouge, Interstate 10. His speed—and his hairy forearms, oyster-blue shirt rolled above the elbows—didn't bless me, but ushered me into unpleasant vertigo. I was frightened by Mr. Petrucci's speed-and-hirsuteness, where Interstate 10 fails to mollify Interstate 12, or fails to conquer it absolutely, like Catherine the Great. I prayed that he would take the Prairieville exit, but he kept speeding on Interstate 10, and my vertigo took the alarming, exciting form of a wish to relieve myself. He eventually arrived in Grosse Tête, where, at a taverna, while Mr. Petrucci and his son Lonny ate gyros, I found my first glory hole."

*

Variety Springs is stained (but not fatally) by former industry; is capable of utopia; is one hour from the Atlantic; is a pocket of economic idealism in a nation headed toward ruin. We have a heavy concentration of healers. Here, home attendants make as much money as lawyers. Not a litigious community. Zen centers, Korean restaurants, kosher butcher, leftist newspaper, a tradition of grass-roots philanthropy and low-level activism. History of accidental electrocutions (live wires). Variety Springs, where amorality reigns. Our mayor sticks up for transgender rights.

My income comes from private practice and guest gigs at healing institutes. I do not seek a permanent appointment. Nor has a search committee approached me.

*

Father: Jacob Kracauer, psychoanalyst. Mother: Bettina Kracauer, psychoanalyst. Sliding scales. I was born in 1964. Only child. Mother had a hysterectomy an unspecified time after my birth. Mother's maiden name: Gold. The one independent gesture I ever made was to leave the Upper West Side, fortress of Kracauer and Gold, and emigrate to Variety Springs.

To discuss: why Tom Cruise's penis has come up in several of my patients' sessions this week.

*

At least I'm not a victim (today) of hypomanic flight of ideas.

Last year Benjamin Levi's lover slashed his wrists in the shower and died. Benjamin's freckled shoulders, light (clipped) hair on upper arms and chest, preference for tank tops, long penis (I've seen it at Baby Snooks Baths).

I need nonstop touch. My father, Jacob Kracauer, hates to be touched. When we hug, he raises one of his shoulders, like a raptor in flight. My mother, Bettina Kracauer (née Gold), specializes in empathy; I inherited none of it. Presence of a nuclear power plant in Westbrook, fifty miles away, gives me nightmares. Bettina would love me to be politically active. I'll work (slowly) toward the political. Maybe I'll become an anti-nuclear activist. Bettina wasn't certain she wanted a child (me); Jacob forced the issue, she said. I can't imagine Jacob forcing.

Killer 69 is my most dangerous client. Dangerous to himself, dangerous to others. Travels with bodyguard. But I don't let him bring the bodyguard into the sessions. I'm trying to talk him out of his paranoid insistence on being accompanied by Bernard, fat bruiser. I'm trying to steer Killer 69's erotic fixation on me into therapeutically useful directions. I limit hands-on erotic work. He trades used vintage sports cars for a living.

*

A stranger whose arm he slugged on the street said to him, "That hurt my arm, when you slugged it." I told Killer 69 to repeat that statement aloud three times. To integrate Killer 69 into polite society *without compromising his radicalism* is our therapy's purpose. Killer 69 is making progress.

*

Killer 69 had a surprising island of insight this afternoon: as I reached my hands beneath the sheet covering his buttocks, he said, "Abandon me." For Killer 69, the combination of abandonment and intrusion is aphrodisiac, and is his closest approximation to what pedestrian minds call "home."

*

Our town bears an indeterminate, pregnant relation to vaudevillian pleasures.

I write these reflections not to advance the cause of arts, letters, or science, but to remain alive (against the contrary, seductive, entropic tide of self-annihilation).

*

Killer 69 told me in his session this morning: "I tricked for the first time with DJ." I pretended impassivity. I didn't tell Killer 69 that I'd had a similar encounter with DJ, a year ago, and that DJ had also told me, "You are exactly my type." I'd wanted him to specify *why I was his type*. He never did.

Sometimes I feel an eviscerating nostalgia for redheads who are cuter versions of me.

*

I am neither a quack nor a malcontent. Notice that my syntax is growing vortex-happy. I am qualified to treat post-traumatic stress disorder, anxiety disorders, disruptive behavior disorders, communication disorders, mood disorders, depression disorders, and sexual and identity disorders. I will never send these ruminations to the Centers for Disease Control or to the Orion Massage Academy in New Fayetteville. My eagerness to hold Killer 69's testicles gives me an adrenaline rush so powerful I'm nearly incapable of completing this sentence, or the next.

*

One week without medication! I'm going cold-turkey off my "tranquilizers." Don't be so inhibited. My parents wanted me to be charming. The purpose of writing is to stave off suicide; my sentences must remain cheerful, factual. To buck up, I should list my good deeds. I'm not a rapist. I give $200 per year to the Variety Springs Jewish Community Center. I don't call the police when I hear Benjamin Levi, downstairs, spanking one of his navvies. Does he rent them, or find them on the streets? How exactly did Pasolini die? How did Siegfried Kracauer die? Killer 69 suffers from oppositional defiant disorder.

*

Vaudeville took root in Variety Springs because no other town in the region (New Fayetteville, Sayreville, Standish, Valhalla Port, Freehold) would tolerate or house it. Only Variety

Springs was spineless enough to accept vaudeville's imbecility. Variety Springs had no identity until vaudeville bestowed one on it. The major vaudeville house in town, Valhalla Palace, gave employment to a wide spectrum of social types, and girded the loins of Variety Springs as a boom town. If Variety Springs ever had a boom, Valhalla Palace was its center. Sophie Tucker played Valhalla Palace. Fanny Brice played Valhalla Palace and haunted the nearby mineral baths. Valhalla Palace, with its pleasing Egyptian-Teutonic exterior, still exists, on Devereux Street, across from the statue of our town's founder, Alexey Devereux. For generations, admission to Valhalla Palace remained a nickel. Now Valhalla Palace is a convention center; but no conventions have seen fit to use the facilities. Valhalla Palace once showed first-run features; then it showed Kung Fu pictures, and porn; now Valhalla Palace hosts the occasional politician, revival meeting, or craft fair, but mostly remains dormant, waiting for a new function.

*

Happy twentieth anniversary of first coitus. Twenty years ago, today: intercourse, finally—after years of propaganda and mystification. It's difficult to write on graph paper. Sounds of spanking downstairs. Last night I put my ear to the floor and heard Benjamin Levi babbling (on the phone?) about terrorism. Either he is planning some terrorist action, or he is having a phobic reaction to recent U.S. history. Benjamin Levi ignores my desirability. On Devereux Street I saw him wearing Birkenstocks and white socks. He has not once made an appointment with me for a massage. I began taking my medicine again last night, unfortunately, so I am once again under the control of Dr. Pellegrino. We'll call it a tranquilizer: a white pill, with a seam down its center, like an incised gut. Chalky taste. The pill gives me a sound sleep and no dreams. My parents don't approve of medications. They are old-fashioned talk therapists.

*

I was silent for an entire year as a child. During my silence, I plotted strategies for changing my personality and my curly red hair, resembling Grandfather Isaac Gold's, whose death would become a frequent dinner-table conversation subject—how to live as survivor of a vaudevillian suicide. I never knew exactly what vaudeville was—that mysterious art at which Isaac Gold had excelled, the art whose obsolescence provoked his suicide. Behind a bathroom door. Push open the door, try to push it open, can't push it open, because Isaac Gold's body, heavy with vaudeville's disappearance, lies behind it. His wife Ludmila Gold, née Kantrowitz, took the death in stride. If I end up killing myself, that's okay. What voice, raised to a certain pitch, doesn't approach suicide?

*

As a youngster I met Marlon Brando. He had begun to get fat. He was sitting in a folding chair in the Poconos—a luxurious resort, where psychotherapists, intellectuals, and actors mingled. Across from him sat Elizabeth Taylor. Rehearsing a scene from *The Glass Menagerie*, they were not embarrassed to be overheard. Brando's face seemed contorted in throes of thespian ecstasy. Soon afterward I saw on TV their live-broadcast version of *Glass Menagerie* (not preserved on tape, it vanished—a great lost performance, Brando playing Tom, Liz playing Laura, though both were too old for the roles); few sources mention their *Glass Menagerie*, which I had the good fortune to see in rehearsal in the Poconos, though Brando might have been rehearsing not with Liz herself but with Liz's stand-in, who looked like Annette Funicello.

*

Behaving like a lunatic won't undo Isaac Gold's suicide. His upper and lower lips weren't aligned, which gave him a shy demeanor, despite his bossiness. "Vaudeville is like Latin," he'd say, "a highly constructed language." "Do you mean that vaudeville is a dead language," I'd ask. "Nonsense," he'd insist; "vaudeville is eternal." "Just like Latin," I'd say. We could go on like that for hours—useless stichomythia. He wanted me to revive vaudeville, and even though I said that "psychotherapy was today's vaudeville" (Bettina agreed), I disappointed him by not "going into" vaudeville, even if going into vaudeville was impossible because it was dead. Shortly before his 1984 suicide, the knowledge of vaudeville's death finally came home to him via a TV broadcast—archival footage of Sophie Tucker's funeral, 1966. He'd attended the ceremony, as had my mother, but he hadn't realized in 1966 that Sophie

Tucker's passing was more than the death of the last of the Red Hot Mamas; it was the death of vaudeville, concentrated in one large body's demise. For the eighteen years separating Sophie Tucker's decease and Isaac Gold's, he never watched one of her movies, even when *Thoroughbreds Don't Cry* or *Gay Love* showed up on the late show. He said, more than once, "It's tragic that Sophie Tucker never became a major film star." "But Isaac," I'd say, "isn't vaudeville superior to cinema?" "Of course," he'd say, "but Sophie Tucker deserved film stardom." Sophie Tucker and my grandfather might have been lovers, though I have no proof; as Bettina put it, "Father kept vaudeville matters under wraps." Indeed, vaudeville specifics were not dinner conversation. "Keep vaudeville vague" was Isaac Gold's motto, and it became Bettina's, as well; vaudeville grandeur was a given, but my grandfather's significance—his place within vaudeville's cosmopolitan yet claustrophobic swirl—remains uncharted, like an imperialist's vision of the Indies in 1489.

*

"Do you know," Bettina Kracauer once said to me, "my revered Melanie Klein died only six years before your grandfather's beloved Sophie Tucker? I'm not sure that Melanie Klein and Sophie Tucker met. Though Melanie Klein probably knew of Sophie Tucker's existence, it's unlikely that Sophie Tucker knew of Melanie Klein, though Klein's work on the psychoanalytic play technique might have had a trickle-down effect on Tucker's rendition of—or her self-perception while rendering—'You've Got To Make It Legal, Mr. Siegel.' When Melanie Klein writes, in 1946, 'The various ways of splitting the ego and internal objects result in the feeling that the ego is in bits,' was she not mourning Sophie Tucker's underpaid labor at the German Village, on Broadway and 40th, in 1906, for a mere $15 a week?"

*

Aeneas's pubic hair forms a flat, high, dark patch—kinky yet clean, organized yet extensive. It matches, in concentration, his face, and has the severity of *Last Year at Marienbad*, a Delphine Seyrig coldness and gravity. Aeneas's pubic patch is black and smug; it ignores small people and strangers. I call it "the Tommy patch." I first saw it in my treatment room. I prefer Tommy—that pubic patch of matte superiority—to Aeneas's penis.

In Baton Rouge and in Lisbon, the Tommy patch had admirers who could not match its immobility, its function as fence. *Don't trample me!* said his groin patch, in Baton Rouge, when it grew to its full breadth, but also in Lisbon, where it first germinated (he left Lisbon at age twelve, when his father died), and where the patch borrowed its airs, its bravura, its identity as shield of Achilles. In Lisbon the patch learned its barricade behavior, though in Baton Rouge it grew to full kingship; then, in Variety Springs, it could look back in complacent awe on its early accomplishments, and it could confidently predict another decade of sovereignty—for Aeneas is only thirty, and his patch, until forty, will be triumphant, at least in my biased eyes. I may be superior to Aeneas in intellect, but Aeneas's patch equalizes us by humbling or humiliating me, when I have the luxury to contemplate it, in the semi-darkness of my treatment room. His Tommy patch can smite me, when it pleases.

*

The Tommy patch counterpoints his gaze. Aeneas's eyes see you, and his Tommy patch sees you. Also his mouth (third item) regards you. Mouth and eyes provide ironic supplement to the Tommy patch. Aeneas can smile or smirk because he knows his Tommy patch immunizes him against your nitpicking. His patch, flat, never vibrates, rises, or assaults. When I see it, I am intrinsically without the tools to measure it. Observing it, I have no choice but to surrender, to live under its Book-of-Hours canopy, its Scrovegni-Chapel tent. (I could never be this explicit in Dr. Pellegrino's presence.) When I first saw Aeneas's Tommy patch I knew I'd found the one object worthy of perpetual attention; I'd found the one zone that would never be kind to me, that would never have my interests at heart.

In Baton Rouge, Aeneas ate crab boil (so he told me) with his mother and his school pals. After spilling crab boil on his white jeans, Aeneas dipped his restaurant napkin in ice water and wiped the stain off his pants at the crotch. The moistened stain, urine-like, gave voice to the confident yet speechless Tommy patch beneath, a Tommy patch that a girl or two had touched, before it became my property.

*

These notes are not escapist exercises, but calisthenics for the political work that will flog Variety Springs "within an inch of its life," as Bettina Kracauer used to say, describing Isaac Gold's spanking act, one of his vaudeville specialties, in which he, playing "The Professor," would spank a dilatory pupil, a girl in a tutu, who compulsively broke into hybrid jazz/ballet moves whenever Isaac ("The Professor") turned his back on the class and wrote mathematical formulae on the chalkboard. The culmination of the spanking act occurred when Isaac commanded his sidekick—victim of a danseuse-Tourette's, a coprolalia of the toeshoe—to stretch herself on Isaac's knee so he could theatrically wallop her, while a cymbal and tympani, in the orchestra pit, crashed and thumped in time with the Professor's handstrokes. At the end of the act, when Isaac once again turned his back, the dancer would re-engage in her jazz/ballet spoof, this time mimicking the Professor. Her dancing replicated Isaac's characteristic, patented waddle; though not corpulent, he shifted his weight from foot to foot as he walked, parodying an obese man's rocking perambulation. Had Isaac Gold once been fat? Or was he paying inverted homage to Sophie Tucker, his beau idéal, and also praising his late mother, Lotte Gold, stern and wide?

I come from a long line of sodomites—the Kracauers and the Golds. My erotic practices pale in comparison to their squalid behavior in clerestories and peanut galleries of vanished vaudeville houses.

*

Today my speech is slow. Slowness stems from sadism. New patient: Hans, seventy years old, heavyset, a Frankfurt art dealer, in town to sample healing waters. I am disgusted by no variety of erotic experience. Hans says he will fly to Bogotá tomorrow to visit his daughter, formerly a kidnapping victim, now a banker. As I massaged his back, Hans told me that his daughter never recovered; she "managed" her feelings, but she never fully "worked them through." I asked if Hans planned to work through *his* feelings. "No, just manage them," said Hans, cheerfully. His stubborn lack of insight appalls me—"a true child of Frankfurt," he proudly calls himself.

*

"Did I ever tell you about my friendship with Paul Bowles?" Bettina said, one night in the Poconos, when I was a teenager. We were, at table, our usual fivesome—Bettina and Jacob Kracauer, me, and Isaac and Ludmila Gold.

Isaac said, "Bettina, I don't know if your son is old enough to hear the Paul Bowles story."

"Nonsense," said Ludmila, "he's nearly a grown man. Look at him."

They all looked at me.

"Do I seem like a grown man?" I asked the assembled four.

"I'm not sure," said Bettina.

"It's definitely a matter of opinion," said Jacob.

"Maturity, like Latin," said Isaac Gold, "is complicated."

"Do you want to hear my Paul Bowles story?" said Bettina.

"We haven't figured out whether our son is mature enough to hear it," said Jacob.

"Let's ask him," said Ludmila.

"I'll ask," said Bettina. "As his mother, I'm the logical candidate."

Everyone fell silent.

Bettina turned to me: "How mature do you feel, Siegfried?"

"I think the Paul Bowles story is too important to tell at dinner table, in a public restaurant," said Jacob.

The next morning, at breakfast, same table, same fivesome, I heard the simple story, not obscene. Bettina, prior to marriage, had gone to Tangier for a psychotherapy conference; Paul Bowles had been keynote speaker. "His talk," Bettina said, "was anti-Freud, anti-psyche. Afterward, I accepted Paul's invitation to return to his apartment, where I heard, for the first time, a recording of Abdelkrim Rais's orchestra playing an Andalusian *nouba*. As you know, Siegfried, there are different *noubas* for different times of the day. Whether Paul played me a morning, afternoon, or evening *nouba*, I don't remember, though I recall that Paul impressed on me the significance of the listener's state of mind, and how that same mood could be simulated afterward without rehearing the *nouba*. Once heard, the *nouba* became a permanent part of your physiology. If only I could sing for you, Siegfried, right here, in the Poconos, that Andalusian *nouba* I first heard in Paul's presence!"

*

My father's upper lip has an opinion about the creation myth and the origin of the species. His upper lip is full (Rita Hayworth) and venal (Mercedes McCambridge or Agnes Moorehead). Are my father's eyes an adult raccoon's or a baby rabbit's? The many Jacob Kracauers coalesce into one scapegoated Green Hornet. Any sentence that describes him is like the long hallway in Cocteau's *Beauty and the Beast*, Bettina's favorite film. Down that paranoid corridor, the frightened beauty, played by Josette Day, wanders, confronted by animate candelabra, each intimating her failure to return home and care for her ailing father. This sentence, here, is the disobedient daughter's drugged refusal to return to the paternal cottage of penury and illness. Writing these words, I remain, ensorcelled and selfish, in the beast's moneyed domain. Too metaphorical!

A Page from My Intimate Journal

Too many of us—the marked, the curiously emblazoned—were crowded together in one room. We would all dwell, for the duration, in a space advertised as ample, though it was in fact a cramped, low-ceilinged attic. Through its windows, we could see defunct factories ranged against the unnaturally orange sky; and we could hear, amid ambulance sirens, the shouts of miscreants, thronged on street corners for cabal and cheerleading. Squatters, grifters, and dubious political organizations now occupied the condemned factories. We attic-dwellers tried to feel superior to the factory-squatters, but we, too, faced squalid circumstances. Forced to sleep five to a bed, and to excrete in slop pots, we received few instructions from our boss: aside from scavenging food-scraps, and generating heat from body contact, we were commanded to scrawl confessions and pleas in the five-by-eight-inch pads with which we were generously supplied, as if these modestly-sized ledgers were a new style of zwieback biscuit.

Sexual misconduct, we knew upon arrival, would infect the attic, where the five-to-a-bed policy deprived us of privacy. As our first task of self-governance, we elected officers for adjudicating cases of sexual wrongdoing, judges who would eject any offenders from premises not luxurious but still preferable to dwelling in unheated factories or on the fume-engulfed streets. As our second task, which would consume the rest of our lives, we began constructing appropriate codes and signals for communicating our plight, and for broadcasting, to future generations, the nature of our five-to-a-bed culture; by carefully limning—in jagged codes—our situation, we might offer guidance to our descendants, should there still be an earth for these unlucky creatures to inhabit.

Our boss, a feared enigma named Rack Gretel, barked out new directions every fifteen minutes. Every quarter-hour, it was time, Rack Gretel said, for us to concoct a new code. Fruitless were our attempts to explain to Rack Gretel that codes could be developed only slowly; hours, months, years, decades are required for codes to germinate, whether composed of fig-leaf or of squirrel-offal. Rack Gretel was a strange slab of human tendency, lacking the clearly defined features of a Popeye or a Pompidou. What Rack Gretel wanted we couldn't discover; all we could discern, and grow to love, was the crude charisma of his tempo, his insistence that all code-creating activities take place at a fast clip.

An emissary—sacrificial, elegant—arose from our five-to-a-bed midst, a comely and ambiguous slip of a girlboy named Careful Last. Careful Last, whose clothing had managed to escape the soiling effects of our straitened circumstance, stepped forward—in a pants-dress, composed of towels, scarves, denim, plastic bags, leather, velvet, and heaps of what even in our pleasure-deprived end-time we still called "attitude"—and offered to carry intelligence of our difficulties to the ears of the factory dwellers, who were, we would soon learn, compelled by their ingenious warlords to invent codes and signals and to inscribe them on five-by-eight-inch pads identical to ours. Careful Last, who had been singled out as the "favorite"—the pampered catamite—of Rack Gretel, took the most refined and the least helpful of our jottings, bundled the pages into a khaki satchel, and took them through the underground tunnel linking our building to the principal factories across the bruising, cabal-haunted thoroughfare. The next day, Careful Last returned, carrying a satchel of factory-generated codes, to our overcrowded domicile.

And so, for months and months, the traffic continued, the daily exchange of codes and signals, from attic to factory, and back again, in the satchel of Careful Last, who became, by virtue of the lightheartedness with which he dispatched his responsibilities, a cult figure. And now, if it is permissible to speak in my own voice, and to express uncouth biases, please let me admit that the fine points of Careful Last's deportment are my primary passion. The pleasure of keeping close watch over Careful's behavior is the only reason I haven't swallowed poison, in these difficult months of parched subsistence and forced code-production.

The same five people do not sleep every night in the same bed; we rotate, according to a system whose niceties and incoherencies are managed by Rack Gretel.

One night, in late January, after the snow had fallen for hours, a blizzard tinted amber by the polluted light through which the flakes traveled, I managed, due to a lapse in Rack Gretel's accounting system (he had fallen asleep over a glass of piney bitters, and I had tampered with his ledger-book), to land a place within Careful Last's bed. Just a moment earlier, Careful Last had returned from the nightly journey through the underground tunnel from factories whose complexities and odiferous horrors I could hardly imagine, and back to an attic that seemed, in comparison, a petit-bourgeois paradise. Beneath the burlap blanket I lay, with three other unnamed, uncared-for code-developers; I could feel Careful Last's slender body slip under the burlap beside me, and so, with a gentleness I feared was criminal, I slithered my body against Careful's. I pressed without genital specificity; neither my genitals, nor Careful's, whatever their nature and composition, had any part in this travelogue. What obtained, between Careful and me, in those last apocalyptic hours, formed a new code we would not in the morning have the temerity or skill to commit to paper, though I can, here, through the medium of oral communication, through groan and whisper and vocal persiflage, tell you a few signal features of our congress.

Careful performed some action on Careful's own body; I witnessed the action, but I did not understand it. I, in response, or in imitation, performed what I hoped was a similar action upon my own body, which was superficially thicker than Careful's body but equally confusing in its characteristics. Careful, however, made no sign to indicate awareness that I was present in the same bed or that I was engaged in a parallel set of enigmatic, graphic, culpable motions, with a robustness almost agricultural. To Careful, I adhered, in my sticky fashion; the stickiness, not a bodily emission, came from my earnestness, as well as from the physical conditions—grease, dust, and other, unsymbolizable forms of particulate dirt—that filled the attic. This impious grime allowed my body to glue itself, with a passé fondness, to uncognizant Careful.

Then a cruel thing happened, and the cruelty was Careful's. Careful enforced a separation, with skills I cannot comprehend, from my resinous body, and pressed closer to another unnamed, unseen personage in our bed. No longer were my limbs and loins receiving Careful's nectar. A sound, wet and soughing, filled the bed; if you have ever heard a refrigerator moaning, when its useful life is almost at an end, then you will understand the noise that Careful made, and how that noise inspired in me a wish to kill Careful. The malevolence arose in me, and I nursed it; but the intent could not communicate itself to my hands. My hands had grown heavy and numb. I tried to wiggle my fingers; they responded only sluggishly. To my hands I bade farewell. This adieu I felt strongly, but I could not communicate it to my body. Whatever system of code-sharing that formerly tied my organism together seemed to have collapsed.

At that moment, Careful turned around and clasped me. Careful kissed me, and though my mouth had no desire to open, I could feel it become a vacancy available to admit Careful's tongue. Careful's tongue, however, was a joke tongue, not quite coterminous with Careful's actual opinions. Careful's tongue attacked me with a spurious directness, a facticity, that undid the wet pink slab's claim: the invader became a *not-quite-tongue*. I therefore had no right to interpret Careful's tongue as a sign of love. The tongue was a taunt. The tongue, though seeming to reward me, to anoint me anew with full-bodied life, and to restore communication between my wishes and my limbs, instead performed a severing. The tongue (if you will forgive my scientism) completed the divorce between cognition and organism.

Careful whispered in my ear, "I deplore what you have done to our system."

"What system?" I whispered in cautious reply.

An unvoiced laugh caused Careful's svelte body to shiver, like a doormat shaken out.

"The system you pretend to uphold, my dear idiot," said Careful.

Careful's candor, and its courtly expression, aroused in me a spasm of religious feeling.

"Could I accompany you tomorrow evening on your mission to the factories?" I asked, as I pressed my body against Careful's.

Toward our bed, Rack Gretel stumbled with a hammer. *Bang bang* went the hammer on the bed's steel rim. Cries arose from every denizen of the attic. Rack Gretel persevered in hammering the bed's rim, with a rhythmic force that reminded me of a brutal passage from *Carmina Burana*, which I had sung in middle school, as a foreign exchange student in a country formerly celebrated for its mathematical and jurisprudential prowess but now mired in baroque webs of corruption.

Wearily, Careful rose. Careful had received the unmistakable summons. Only to Careful did the summons—the hammering blows—refer. The hammer's retort *signified* Careful, as the logicians would formerly have said, in the highly literate country where I had the honor to be a foreign exchange student, although I was later expelled from school and sent back to my own country because of an infraction I'd committed with the school's dean. The dean condemned me, though we had been involved together in this carnal misdeed, whose source, as always, lay in the soft areas concealed by belts and sashes.

For the rest of the night, only four people occupied the bed where recently Careful and I had undergone our peculiar procedure. I don't want to stop telling you the story of Careful and me, of Careful and our civilization, of Careful and the ogre Rack, of the warehouses and the orange sky and the sweaty beds. I don't want to stop inscribing codes in the five-by-eight-inch pads. I don't want Careful to be punished. I want Careful to keep undertaking the perilous journey through the tunnel, nightly, to circulate intelligence of the codes and signals our two populations are heretically inscribing in our allotted pads. Always, at the end of a story, the story shuts itself down, as if the story were punishing itself for being a story, as if the codes were killing themselves because it was criminal to be a code.

The next morning, Rack served me a bowl of porridge. I hadn't tasted porridge since my internment began. Kindness toward me, a kindness exercised by Rack, could only mean that Careful had been destroyed. A new softness, a new unctuousness and solicitude on Rack's part, meant that Careful's gracile, malarial ambiguities had been banished—whatever mortal injury a Rack-style banishment entailed. "Stop belly-aching about Careful," you might say. "Didn't you want to kill

Careful, a few hours ago?" And so continues the cruel march of chronology, of *logos*, as my old nurse used to whimper, before shipping me off to the penal farm. "There goes *logos*," Nurse would say, his whiskers brushing against my too-logical forehead. Before I left Nurse's care, we together manufactured an ointment, vaguely medicinal. We developed a brochure to advertise the salubrious effects of our greasy concoction, and we sold the ointment to gullible travelers who frequented our hamlet, buried in a region far from the most popular rivers but near a lagoon crowded in all seasons with festive houseboats, some of them functioning not only as vacation properties but as haute-bourgeois restaurants. Nurse and I had the wit to escape responsibility for the atrocities that might have ensued from a too-sanguine or too-literal application of the ointment we sloppily produced.

The sound of a siren, outside the attic, splits open the atmosphere. I look down from the attic window and see the factories consumed by flames. Good night to codes and signals, to Careful and Rack. Good night to the rivalry between factories and attic. Good night to recollections of ointments purchased by houseboat-visitors in the golden age before my multiple, unspecified expulsions. I am not immune to the disasters I describe. Purge that sentimental observation from the official record.

Acknowledgments

Thank you, Hedi El Kholti, for believing in my idiom. Thank you, Janique Vigier, for ushering Semiotext(e) books, including mine, into the world. PJ Mark, thank you for sweetly steering me. Thank you to all the writers and artists and friends who have encouraged my visual and verbal explorations. And thank you to all my students, present and past, who guide me toward new, cheerful postures of experiment and play.

Special thanks to the editors of the following publications, and the artists and curators of the following exhibitions and occasions, for giving these fables a first home:

"The Cheerful Scapegoat" is forthcoming in *More Than a Manifesto* (Essay Press), edited by Dorothea Lasky.

"The Cheerful Scapegoat in the Suburbs" was published in *Failed States: a journal of indeterminate geographies* (*issue #2: suburb*), edited by Jamie Atherton.

"The Cheerful Scapegoat (We Three)" was published in *Solitary Pleasures*, edited by Marquard Smith (Live Art Development Agency, 2018), in conjunction with the exhibition *Solitary Pleasures* at the Freud Museum (London), 2018, curated by Smith.

"Pulling Lashes," "Gardener's Scarf," "That Odd Summer of '84," "Sorting Out Andy," and "Bloomsbury Revisited" appeared in *The Paris Review* (#227, Winter 2018), in conjunction with paintings by Hernan Bas.

"Green Ice Cream Man I Didn't Love," "And Then I Threw My Hands in the Air," "The Terror of Complications," and "Telephone Receivers or Cooking Spoons in Purple Haze" appeared in *Pioneer Works Journal*, alongside photographs by Jimmy DeSana, thanks to the editorial invitation of David Everitt Howe.

"The Snow Falls On...," "Pincushion with Thimble," "Zucchini Blossoms," "Gay Memphis Bookcase," "Reverse Butterfly," and "The Greenhouse" appeared in a limited-edition artist's book, *Paintings and Fables*, featuring the paintings of Eric Hibit, in 2017.

"Dimples in His Tie," "Martha Never Asked Permission Before Dropping By," "Thrown Crystal," "Terrifying Typo," "The Logic of Rivulets," and "He Is Perpetually Tan" appeared in a limited-edition chapbook published by Margaret Tedesco at [2nd floor projects], San Francisco, 2017. The chapbook was part of an exhibition featuring the art of Josh Faught and Katherine Vetne.

"The Temple of Timidity," "Profile of a Departed Cellist," "Do You Take Mustard?," "Decor Analysis," "An Exercise in Expiation," and "Conversation in Darkness" are forthcoming in *Black Mirror*, a book regarding the artist Monica Majoli, edited by Sabrina Tarasoff.

"Pillow and Tom," "Newspaper on a Dubious Patio," "Mayoral Chandelier," and "The Diplomatic Rock" appeared in *Stories of Almost Everyone*, edited by Aram Moshayedi, published by the Hammer Museum (Los Angeles), in conjunction with an exhibition curated by Moshayedi (with Ikechukwu Onyewuenyi) in 2018.

HOR

—poet, critic, novelist, artist, performer—
-one books, including *Figure It Out, Camp
80s & Other Essays, The Anatomy of Harpo
Hotel Theory, Circus, Andy Warhol, Jackie
d The Queen's Throat* (nominated for a
ics Circle Award). In 2020 he received an
of Arts and Letters Award in Literature. His
Yale's Beinecke Rare Book and Manuscript
tinguished Professor of English, French, and
ature at the City University of New York

"Sebald Sandwich" appeared in *Imaginary Oklahoma*, edited by Jeff Martin, and published in Tulsa by This Land Press, 2013.

"Who Speaks?" appeared in *qui parle* (December 2017).

"The Pathos of Communication" appeared in *The Pathos of Communication*, a project edited by Richard Milazzo, in *OBSzine* (September 2017).

"To Be Engulfed," "Disreality," and "Declaration" appeared in issue #5 of *Fireflies*, edited by Annabel Brady-Brown and Giovanni Marchini Camia, in a portfolio of pieces honoring Agnès Varda; these three fables were inspired by her first film, *La Pointe Courte*.

"Stones and Liquor: or, Some Differences between Remorse and Regret," "A Few Don'ts about Yellow Wallpaper," "Pink Eye (A Family Romance)," "On Not Being Able to Paint," and "The Artist's Methods" were commissioned by the Renaissance Society, at the University of Chicago, in conjunction with Alejandro Cesarco's 2017 exhibition *Song*, at the editorial invitation of the artist and Karsten Wales Lund. The first three of these fables were subsequently published in a book, *Song*, edited by Cesarco, and published in 2018 by the Renaissance Society.

"Variety Springs" was published in *Between Men: Best New Gay Fiction*, edited by Richard Canning, and published by Carroll & Graf, 2007.

"A Page from My Intimate Journal" was commissioned by Jacob Robichaux and Sam Gordon, for Gordon Robichaux Gallery, New York City, as part of the exhibition *A Page from My Intimate Journal (Part I)*, in 2018.

ABOUT THE AUT

Wayne Koestenbaum
has published twent
Marmalade, My 19
Marx, Humiliation,
Under My Skin, a
National Book Cri
American Academy
literary archive is a
Library. He is a Dis
Comparative Liter
Graduate Center.

ABOUT THE AUTHOR

Wayne Koestenbaum—poet, critic, novelist, artist, performer—has published twenty-one books, including *Figure It Out, Camp Marmalade, My 1980s & Other Essays, The Anatomy of Harpo Marx, Humiliation, Hotel Theory, Circus, Andy Warhol, Jackie Under My Skin,* and *The Queen's Throat* (nominated for a National Book Critics Circle Award). In 2020 he received an American Academy of Arts and Letters Award in Literature. His literary archive is at Yale's Beinecke Rare Book and Manuscript Library. He is a Distinguished Professor of English, French, and Comparative Literature at the City University of New York Graduate Center.

"Sebald Sandwich" appeared in *Imaginary Oklahoma*, edited by Jeff Martin, and published in Tulsa by This Land Press, 2013.

"Who Speaks?" appeared in *qui parle* (December 2017).

"The Pathos of Communication" appeared in *The Pathos of Communication*, a project edited by Richard Milazzo, in *OBSzine* (September 2017).

"To Be Engulfed," "Disreality," and "Declaration" appeared in issue #5 of *Fireflies*, edited by Annabel Brady-Brown and Giovanni Marchini Camia, in a portfolio of pieces honoring Agnès Varda; these three fables were inspired by her first film, *La Pointe Courte*.

"Stones and Liquor: or, Some Differences between Remorse and Regret," "A Few Don'ts about Yellow Wallpaper," "Pink Eye (A Family Romance)," "On Not Being Able to Paint," and "The Artist's Methods" were commissioned by the Renaissance Society, at the University of Chicago, in conjunction with Alejandro Cesarco's 2017 exhibition *Song*, at the editorial invitation of the artist and Karsten Wales Lund. The first three of these fables were subsequently published in a book, *Song*, edited by Cesarco, and published in 2018 by the Renaissance Society.

"Variety Springs" was published in *Between Men: Best New Gay Fiction*, edited by Richard Canning, and published by Carroll & Graf, 2007.

"A Page from My Intimate Journal" was commissioned by Jacob Robichaux and Sam Gordon, for Gordon Robichaux Gallery, New York City, as part of the exhibition *A Page from My Intimate Journal (Part I)*, in 2018.